IN GRAVES BELOW

A Magic, New Mexico Story

CAROL VAN NATTA

Can a disabled veteran and a magical dancer learn the secret of dreamwalk, or will demons turn the world into an all-you-can-eat buffet?

Disabled, scarred veteran **Idrián Odair** is running out of time. If he doesn't figure out how to renew the magical barrier protecting his tribal lands near Magic, New Mexico soon, they'll be vulnerable to marauders, thieves, and worst of all, tourists. Trouble is, his grandfather died before telling him the secret, and Idrián is the only dreamwalk warrior left. Except for the stunning dancer he saw only once and can't forget.

Riya Sanobal, mostly human dancer in Denver, is about to be named artistic director of a dance company. She can't stop thinking about the sexy, eagle-footed warrior she's been dreaming about for weeks. Especially since she's stuck with an obnoxious visiting star and a big donor with a mega sleaze factor.

When Idrián's grandfather insists Idrián must drive to Denver to protect the dancer, finding her turns out to be the easy part. A powerful, greedy demon wants to invite more of his kind to town to make the world an all-you-can-eat buffet. He needs a dancer to do it, and he's targeted Riya. If the discovers Riya's gift for portal magic, he'll never let her go.

Not if Idrián can help it. But even spiriting Riya away to his New Mexico home won't save them if they can't figure out the secret of dreamwalk.

Note to Readers: This is a re-release of a story originally published in the Magic, NM Kindle Worlds program.

ALSO BY CAROL VAN NATTA

Paranormal Romance

- Shifter Mate Magic (Ice Age Shifters #1)
- Shift of Destiny (Ice Age Shifters #2)
- Heart of a Dire Wolf (Ice Age Shifters #3)
- Dire Wolf Wanted (Ice Age Shifters #4)
- Ice Age Shifters Collection Books 1-4

- In Graves Below (Magic, NM)

Space Opera - Central Galactic Concordance Series

- Last Ship Off Polaris-G (Novella)
- Overload Flux (Book 1)
- Minder Rising (Book 2)
- Zero Flux (Novella)
- Pico's Crush (Book 3)
- Pet Trade (Novella)
- Jumper's Hope (Book 4)
- Cats of War (Novella)
- Spark Transform (Book 5)
- Central Galactic Concordance Box Set Books 1-3

Retro Science Fiction Comedy

- Hooray for Holopticon

FOREWORD FROM S.E. SMITH

Imagine The Worlds of Magic, New Mexico...

A series that brings together outstanding paranormal and science fiction authors to expand a town where witches, aliens, vampires, werewolves, goblins, sorceresses, pirates, time travelers, and paranormal live in harmony—when they aren't joining forces to defeat the bad guys. A magical town where being abnormal is the norm!

I'm S.E. Smith, the creator of Magic, New Mexico and I invite you to curl up with each book now and discover all the action, the magic, and the love that makes Magic, New Mexico the ultimate go-to series for Paranormal / Science Fiction Romance readers.

For all the stories, go to MagicNewMexico.com/books/. Grab your copy today!

Thanks to my brave and loyal beta readers, my professional editor Shelley Holloway of Holloway House, and my very talented cover designer Melody Simmons.

Special thanks to Susan Smith, who was kind enough to invite me to participate in the Magic, New Mexico adventure.

T HE LITTLE BELLS on the door played a cheerful tune as another customer walked in the noisy, crowded Hungry Hippogryph diner in Magic, New Mexico. A magical spell caused the bells to play a unique melody for each person who entered.

Idrián Odair was having one of those mornings. All his errands in town, from stopping at the feed store for special kibble, to getting his mail and buying groceries, to dropping off tourist-trade sand paintings at the gallery for summer consignment sales, had taken longer than planned. Now it was noon, and the diner and its front waiting area were packed. He'd nearly turned around and left, but the other restaurants would be just as busy, and he was hungry for anything he didn't have to cook for himself.

The diner was popular with the town locals because the owner catered to the unusual tastes and nutritional needs of its customers. Most were magical, and some weren't even remotely human. The restaurant was equally popular with human tourists because of its kitschy decor and relaxed ambiance. Powerful illusion and protection spells in the town made peaceable mingling of the locals and the tourists possible by convincing tourists they saw only ordinary people, not magical beings of their fairy tales, myths, and nightmares.

"Hey, Idrián," said a wide, tall, and heavy dwarf-ogre male, "long time no see." His deep and rumbling voice sounded like grinding gravel, and his oversized hands and arms could tear apart a small car if he was of a mind, but he was the kindest, gentlest being Idrián had ever met. He was only eighty years old, which was barely out of adolescence for either dwarves or ogres.

"Heya, Warrk," Idrián said with a smile. "When did you get back?" Last Idrián had heard, his friend had been at a six-month-long family reunion organized by his parents, who had a hidden island to themselves off the coast of Denmark. Warrk had enough siblings, nieces, and nephews to populate a small city.

Warrk smiled. "Couple of weeks ago. Glad to be back where it's warm." His smile faded. "Sorry to hear about Black Fox. You must miss him."

Idrián nodded. "I do, and thank you." It had been five months since his grandfather had died unexpectedly, and his spirit had yet to appear anywhere. Unlike most tribal traditions of the region, his people cherished the spirits of the dead, rather than fearing them.

A male behind Idrián laughed. "As much as he liked to be in everyone's business, you'd think he'd have come back the next day."

Idrián turned carefully to see his friend Rollie, a native

coyote shifter, grinning at him. Rollie could have passed for an ordinary human, except for his sharp golden eyes and even sharper, permanently pointed teeth.

"True," agreed Idrián, "but he liked doing the unexpected even more. He's probably waiting for the perfect moment."

He hoped it was soon, because Black Fox To'Piro had left unfinished business. He'd died before explaining how to access the protective wards around the family ranch and mesh them with the wards of Magic. Both were due to be renewed in a week, in preparation for the coming onslaught of summer tourists. Early birds were already showing up, like the noisy group in the big corner booth near the counter. Pretty soon, the town would be overrun. After Idrián dealt with the wards problem, he planned to hide out for the rest of the season. The ranch was both his therapy and his refuge.

The diner's front door opened to admit Rollie's long-time mate and new husband, Hanif, a magician and jackal shifter who'd fled persecution in Egypt a couple of centuries earlier. Hanif looked like a shy version of Doctor Zhivago from the movie of the same name. Rollie stood to greet Hanif with a kiss, then motioned Idrián to take his seat.

Ordinarily, Idrián would have refused, but he was having a bad day with his legs. The new brace for his right leg still rubbed him raw in one spot, and his left, below-the-knee stump, was itching under the liner for his prosthetic leg. He used his cane to lever himself carefully into the chair. He couldn't afford another fall like he'd had last week.

Hanif tapped Rollie's arm. "Tell Idrián about Yelena and the others."

At Idrián's questioning look, Rollie said, "Yelena's been having bad dreams again, and so have Louis and Harrigan."

The common denominator between them was their war-veteran status—Yelena from Iraq, Louis from Vietnam, and Harrigan from World War II. Rollie had served in Iraq, and Idrián in both Iraq and Afghanistan.

"What about you?" asked Idrián.

"Only good dreams, but Hanif's magic might be protecting me." Rollie smiled and nudged Hanif playfully. "Glad I married a Magic man." Hanif blushed. They were both still enjoying the novelty of being able to legally marry like everyone else.

"I'll look into it," promised Idrián.

A month ago, he'd discovered a brazen fear-eater demon in the underworld dreamwalk plane tending and nurturing dreamer fears, instead of eating them. It violated the negotiated agreements made long ago between his ancestors and the various demon realms. Idrián came close to losing the fight until a clever, feather-haired, drop-dead gorgeous woman had appeared and helped him defeat the big demon. After their victory, before he could ask her name, she'd kissed him. The kiss had aroused every cell in his body and nearly made him forget his *own* name, and then she'd vanished.

The memory of it aroused him in the real world, too, leaving him hard and aching at inconvenient times. Even though he'd searched the dreamwalk practically every night for the past four weeks as he'd made his rounds, he hadn't found her again.

In the old days, the dreamwalk plane had been guarded by dozens of medicine man and spider woman ancestors to keep greedy demons from using it as a gateway to the real world, where humans would become an all-you-can-eat buffet for insatiable demon appetites. Idrián was the last of his tribe to patrol the dreamwalk, and even though he visited every night, he couldn't be everywhere at once.

Warrk, Rollie, and Hanif invited him to join them in the narrow booth that became available, but Idrián declined in favor of a seat at the counter, which was easier for him to maneuver in and out of. Unfortunately, it was also near the big booth occupied by the tourists, who noticed him immediately. He knew their sudden silence and subsequent whispering were about him.

He was hard to look at, with the burn scars on the left side of his head, a drooping left eye, and deformed ear. Where the hair no longer grew on the burned side of his skull, he wore an intricate, stylized tattoo of an eagle in flight. He wore the rest of his long, straight black hair in a braid down his back. Like so many of his fellow disabled veterans, he'd been the victim of a roadside bomb, and lived to tell the tale. Knowing he'd been lucky to live didn't make it any easier to be stared at like a freak-show exhibit.

Zola, the pretty, smiling waitress, took his order for a big burger and fries, then brought him a glass of iced tea with two lemons while he waited. He also ordered a large salad to go, which would be a nice treat for when he got home.

Chores had stacked up at the ranch while he'd recovered from his twisted back, the result of his fall when trying to perform a sacred dance. His damaged body just wasn't up to the task any more, and the dance was the only way he knew to access the ranch's protective wards, which had been keyed to his now-deceased grandfather. Without them, the ranch would soon be overrun with grave robbers, sorcerers, and, worst of all, tourists.

The whispering at the table of outsiders grew more animated. Idrián tried to tune it out, but there was nothing wrong with his hearing.

"...thought all Indians lived on the reservation..."

"...carrying your gun, aren't you? If he has PTSD, he might go crazy..."

"...to be called Indians. You're supposed to call them Native Americans..."

"...if he's even a veteran. Probably a drunk-driving accident or something. Indians are all alcoholics."

"...that face, when decent people are trying to eat..."

Idrián closed his eyes a moment and forced his shoulders to relax, then focused on the list of things he needed to do when he got home.

Zola cleared her throat to get his attention, then slid his plate in front of him. She'd only been in Magic for a few years, and had blossomed in a town where she could be herself. She had a sweet, sympathetic face, light brown skin, and a slight Cajun accent. Her eyes were a startling milky white, and while she was conventionally blind, she had mysterious magic that let her see far better than sighted folk.

"Idrián," she said, giving his Spanish name a distinctly French pronunciation, "why don't you use the conceal-ment glamour the town council offered? Then idiots like those ignorant jackasses in the corner won't bother you."

He shook his head. "I can't. I still have to visit the normal world, and I'd have to get used to people's reactions all over again. I need the reminder of what people really think of me."

Zola put her hand on his where it was wrapped tightly around his iced-tea glass. "I see a big heart, *cher*, made for love. Don't let what happened with Bianca Jacobs convince you that's what everyone else sees. She was a greedy, self-interested bitch with a cruel streak as wide as the Rio Grande. I'm damn glad she was disinvited."

Idrián cracked a half smile. "Tell me how you really felt about her, Zola."

"I would, except my mama raised me better than that." She unerringly poured more iced tea for him and left to take care of other customers.

His heart had been battered by a blonde bombshell of a woman who'd blown into Magic, used up her welcome, and vanished, but not before she'd made a play for him and convinced him she saw the real man underneath the ruined façade. He'd been so caught up in the dream of finding someone who could love him that he'd ignored the inconvenient facts. Such as, she hated being touched, had no underworld dreamwalk talent, and was inordinately interested in the vein of sorcerer's silver that ran through the tribal ranch's biggest mountain. Her primary magic was making people see what they wished for.

He also should have suspected trouble when Black Fox, who had strong, vocal opinions on everything under the sun, refused to say what he thought about his grandson's choice in a girlfriend. Bianca revealed her true nature and burned her bridges before she got her claws on anything important, but it had been a painful and important lesson in bitter-cold reality.

He put the experience out of his mind and focused on eating the really good burger and perfectly cooked fries Zola had just delivered. Maybe he'd finally find the gorgeous, kissing woman when he visited the dreamwalk that night.

2

I DRIÁN DROVE HIS deceptively ugly and beat-up pickup truck past the yard's first gate and let it close before pressing the separate remote to open the inner gate to the enclosed yard. The automatic gate controls had been well worth the expense, and the dual-gate system saved him from chasing animals that viewed gates as an exciting game.

As Idrián unloaded the supplies from the truck onto the attached cart of the big-tired, all-terrain vehicle that a veteran's charity had found for him, he sent his earth magic out across the ranch's several hundred acres to check on the status of the northeast fence line. Thanks to his heritage and magical gifts, he had a bone-deep connection to the soil and could feel every plant and animal on it. The land had become sacred centuries ago and contained the remains of many of his magical ancestors.

When the Spanish conquistadors arrived in the late 1500s, as Europeans counted time, the native medicine men, spider women, and dreamwalkers of the farming Tompiro and nomadic Jumano peoples formed an alliance. They moved west to claim a flat plain and a few mountains, and protected them all with magic. They couldn't protect themselves from internal disagreements or European diseases, however, so the population and territory had steadily shrunk.

In the 1700s, when the town of Magic was founded, the reclusive blended tribe recognized kindred magic spirits who longed for the freedom to be left alone. They formed a mutual protection alliance that thrived, even though the tribe continued to diminish. The native spirits remained strong and plentiful in graves below, which was why the land was still protected, but now Idrián, his cousin Román, and their mothers were the only living members left. His grandfather's radical choice to marry a dreamwalk partner who happened to be a half-white, half-Chinese woman from San Francisco had scandalized his spirit ancestors, but they'd conceded the tribe would be as extinct as their language if both Black Fox and his sister hadn't bucked tradition.

Idrián shut the truck's tailgate, then drove the ATV into the barn, the largest building on the property. He knew his friends thought he lived a silent, lonely life on the ranch. He snorted. They didn't know his spirit ancestors.

"The northeast fence is broken," complained T'loc'til, an ancient-looking, barefoot man who only manifested a loincloth because the other spirits complained when he bent over.

"Yes," agreed Idrián. He greeted the patient pinto horse he and his grandfather had raised from an orphaned foal. The pinto directed soft, questing horse lips toward his chest pocket, hoping to find a treat. "In a minute, Patli."

Necalli, the firecat he was permanently fostering for the Touch of Magic animal shelter, twined about his legs once and trilled. She smelled the charcoal kibble he'd picked up from the feed store, but was too polite to raid the bags while he was looking. She proudly sent him an image of singeing the tails of a couple of were-wolf cubs. Young shifters had permission to roam the tribal land, but they weren't allowed to hurt any of the animals or be destructive. Necalli enjoyed enforcing the rules.

Two of the goats pretended to threaten the half dozen feral jackalopes that had come inside the barn to see if he'd brought them anything. The antlered rabbits arose from a legendary incident in Magic, and a fair number of them had taken refuge on the ranch. They ate exotic, invasive brush the goats wouldn't touch, and made a good defense system. Idrián dumped the takeout salad into several bowls and set them out.

The spirit of plain-faced but cheerful Juana Morales drifted into view. "I think the living space would look nice with new curtains." Thanks to her water-witch powers, the ranch had enjoyed a magical source of underground water since the early 1900s, even during droughts. Idrián tried to conserve it, though, because it was still the edge of the desert.

"It doesn't have any curtains now," said Idrián.

"My point exactly," said Juana, beaming. "I'll meditate on what color they should be." She drifted away.

"You didn't go into town to drink again, did you?"

asked Moyolhuani, a short, faded spirit woman from centuries ago.

"Oh, leave him alone," said her husband, Citlali, only slightly taller and equally faded. "He got drunk once when he was seventeen. He didn't even drink after that pale-haired *uxtl'nòc'tli ji'tclan* thought she could steal the ranch."

"Language," chided Moyolhuani. "Even though I agree she was a nasty corn blight. Idrián, did you remember the cooking oil?"

Idrián put away the groceries and worked steadily for the rest of the afternoon on his chores, accompanied by dozens of chatty, opinionated spirits. It was the legacy of all dreamwalkers to be able to see and interact with ghosts anywhere, but especially on tribal lands. He really wished his cousin Román would come home and take on his share of the ranch duties, or at least be someone else for the ancestor spirits to talk to.

He was looking forward to his nightly patrol down under in dreamwalk. It was peaceful and quiet, except for a spirit bird and the complex rhythms that the winds made. If that same fear-eater demon was nosing about, he'd banish it permanently to its own dimension. Maybe that would bring the gorgeous woman again. If it did, this time, he'd initiate the kissing. In the real world, he'd never be so bold, but in dreamwalk, he'd battle a horde of hungry demons for the chance to take that woman to his bed.

In dreamwalk, Idrián twirled and stamped his right foot,

completing the intricate pattern that reinforced the dreamwalk magic protecting his ancestors, thankful that his dreamwalk self didn't have the disabilities of his flesh-and-blood body. He took one last breath of dreamwalk, then looked up and slowly rose in the air toward the deep red sky with blue stars that morphed into grains of multi-colored sands as he passed through them. His patrol had been quiet, yielding neither recalcitrant demons nor sexy women.

Dreamwalk was malleable and huge, even his people's claimed portion of it, so he could have just been in the wrong place at the wrong time. Just like he'd been in Afghanistan, where a roadside bomb had vaporized his lower left leg and foot. The dreamwalk-manifested graves of his ancestors were clean and orderly, but they wouldn't stay that way if demons ever figured out he was the only living dreamwalker on patrol.

He flowed up through the familiar earth and rejoined with his body, sprawled comfortably in the soft soil of the tribe's underground kiva. It felt like sliding into a warm blanket, dried by the noonday sun. He exhaled the last of the dreamwalk essence, then inhaled the air of Earth. The room was still and blissfully quiet. It was as relaxed as he'd felt in days.

"Still sleeping your life away, Eaglefoot?"

Idrián's eyes flew open as he sat up fast. "Black Fox?" He looked around, wondering if it was just wishful think-ing, or a remnant of a waking dream from the part of his mind that stayed in the real world. "Grandfather?"

Like right out of a Hollywood movie, a miniature storm formed at the north edge of the round kiva space and grew into billowing, black thunderclouds, complete with blowing dust and miniature lightning that struck the side wall and left tiny singe marks. The turbulent clouds billowed and swelled into the ghostly form of his grandfather, wearing his favorite jeans, western-patterned chamois shirt, and turquoise-beaded headband.

Idrián bowed his head, then looked up with a grin. "Flashy."

Black Fox tried to look thunderous, but the corner of his mouth twitched, acknowledging Idrián's appreciation for the dramatic entrance. "How long have I been gone?"

"Five months." Idrián pulled on the silicone socket liner and a sock, then reached for his prosthesis. It looked like a wire-form model of a leg, built with carbon fiber and magic by his friend Warrk, with just the right amount of weight to make Idrián feel balanced, and a socket that magically adapted to his stump as it swelled and shrank during the day. He carefully wiped any dust out of the socket before pulling it onto his stump. "Where have you been?"

"Time moves differently in the spirit world, much worse than dreamwalk." Black Fox stared determinedly at his left arm, which was fading in and out like a strobe. "It's harder than you think to manifest something the living can see." The arm diffused, then stabilized. "The others tell me it'll be months before I can make non-dreamwalkers see me."

"I thought you might be looking for Miàoyīng." Black Fox's beloved wife had died in a freak, fiery accident twenty years ago, when Idrián was ten. That her spirit had never come back to the land had hurt Black Fox's feelings deeply, though he'd never admit it.

Black Fox looked peevish. "I will look for her soon, but my living grandson has unfinished business."

Idrián was determined not to let his grandfather rile him. He carefully levered himself up and onto his feet, then brushed the dirt off the back of his pants before grabbing his cane. Now that he was standing again, his hips and back muscles reminded him that he'd probably overdone it that day, and would need to pop a couple of anti-inflammatory pills to get any sleep. He didn't like taking them, but he'd never figured out how to use his earth magic to heal himself in the real world. He was afraid he'd never be the medicine man his grandfather had been. "Tell me what to do about the wards."

"Have you found your dreamwalk partner yet? You need her help." When Idrián rolled his eyes, Black Fox crossed his arms. "Have you done *any* of the three simple tasks I asked of you?" He ticked them off on ghostly fingers. "Train dreamwalk warriors? Find your dreamwalk partner? Make babies?"

"*Simple* tasks?" sputtered Idrián, despite his best intention to stay calm. He held up a finger. "No warriors to train, unless you count one fear-eater demon." He held up a second finger. "Haven't met her, and yes, I've looked." He held up his thumb. "See previous answer."

"What do you mean, haven't met her?" growled Black Fox. "What about that woman in your dreamwalk, a month ago? She has nice, wide, childbearing hips and large breasts for milk. She could handle twins. She was very hot for you."

Idrián fought not to grind his teeth. "How could you know about her, if you weren't here yet? Oh, never mind. It doesn't matter, because I haven't seen her since."

Idrián marched toward the stairs that led out of the sacred space. In ancient times, the tribe had used wooden ladders, but his family had installed a stair unit decades ago, to make it easier for Idrián's elderly great-grand-mother, a formidable spider woman and dreamwalker in her day, to get in and out. Despite his annoyance, Idrián took his time, making sure his feet were placed correctly on each step. One of the many little things he'd taken for granted before his incident was getting feedback from his legs without having to look.

He stepped up into the mobile home's cozy space, then closed the trap door and whispered the words of the spell that made the outline vanish. It was handy having witches in Magic who'd trade spells for useful ingredients found on hallowed ground.

Black Fox rose through the solid floor. "She probably didn't come back because you didn't teach her how. You were too busy kissing her. That alone should have told you she's the partner you have been waiting for, not a certain evil blonde vulture with cold eyes and skinny hips."

"Fine. I'm doomed to be alone. The dreamwalk will be overrun with demons that will destroy our people's graves on their way to Earth, and the tribe will die when I die. Go bother Román."

Idrián turned away and walked to the kitchen, where he kept his meds. It might take months to get a VA hospital appointment or a treatment plan, but at least it was easy to refill prescriptions online. He knocked two pills into his palm and washed them down with the last swallows of cold coffee from his morning cup. He never wasted water if he could help it.

He leaned against the counter and glared at his grandfather.

"You're too stubborn for your own good," grumbled Black Fox.

Idrián snorted. "As stubborn as the *Káhá Tsiní* who chose not to teach me about the wards or about how to find living people in dreamwalk, because I 'wasn't ready.'" His grandfather's private family nickname meant "armadillo" in the almost-extinct Piro language, and for good reason. Their ancestral stories said armadillos didn't like to do anything that wasn't their idea, and grew their armor to make it hard for anyone to make them.

Black Fox frowned sourly. "Fine. We are both stubborn men." It was as close to an apology as Black Fox ever came.

He drifted closer to Idrián and tried unsuccessfully to put a hand on his shoulder. "The Tompiro Spider Woman gave me a prophecy for you. She said your way to the earth is with the dreamwalk woman who conjures the key, and that she's in danger and needs you. Tomorrow. Now. Yesterday. What do you know about her?"

The Tompiro Spider Woman's ability to see the future had saved both her people and the Jumano tribe from the Spanish slavers. Since having come back as a spirit, she only delivered prophecies concerning critical matters, such as the importance of the tribe welcoming the founders of the town of Magic, or a warning about the coming Civil War. Idrián was both honored and alarmed that she bestirred herself for him.

He thought back to the dreamwalk fight. "She wears feathers like she was born with them. She's handy with a slingshot. She's a dancer—she thought she was lucid dreaming the solution to her choreography problem." Her unseen vibrant energy had drawn his focus like a magnet and distracted him from the battle with the big fear-eater demon. He was already losing, and would have been defeated if he'd seen her beautifully muscular, hourglass figure and stunning face during the fight. He wasn't going to admit any of that to his grandfather.

Her words came bubbling up from his memory. "She said something about 'the Mile High City.' I think she lives in Denver."

"Then we must drive the truck to Denver immediately."

The Spider Woman's prophecy was important, but the most convincing argument was that Black Fox was willing to travel, something he hated more than anything.

Idrián would have to make arrangements for Rollie and Hanif to come tend to his animals, a favor they'd done for him before. And if Idrián didn't find time to get at least a couple of hours of sleep, Black Fox would have to learn to manifest in the real world enough to do the driving.

3

T HE LITHE, HEROIC male dancer leapt high into the air and executed a perfect sweeping kick against his opponent, a flexible male dancer with sly, demonic body movements. The angle of the staging made it look like the hero raked a clawed foot across the demon's chest, and the demon contorted with convincing pain.

"Yes, that's it, Mack. Now I believe your talons are weapons, not just costume decoration." Riya Sanobal gave the blond a thumbs-up sign. "The costume ladies promise they'll have the feathered leggings ready for tomorrow night. You'll look great." Even in a long, black wig, he wouldn't look as darkly handsome or amazingly sexy as the painted warrior from her dreams, but audiences loved Mack.

She turned to the other male dancer, Kenji, a wiry Japanese man. "Perfect timing on the reaction. Twist a little more stage left on the recovery. Let's make sure even the cheap seats get to see the blood, since we've gone to all the trouble to rig it." Kenji grinned and patted the rehearsal chest piece he was wearing. They'd load it up with fake blood for the performances, to make it look like Mack's taloned feet were really doing damage. Kenji's talent would sell it.

"One more time," she announced, "to set it in your bodies. We'll go right through to the end, unless Whitney misses with all her rocks."

She reset the rehearsal music to a few bars before the sequence they were working on. As the male dancers listened for their cue, Whitney subtly twitched a finger to the beat, counting. She was a self-described ballet refugee from a prestigious company back East that could never seem to find even a supporting role for a tall, athletic African-American woman, no matter how talented she was. Ballet's loss was the Maruaway Dance Theater Company's gain. She was just coming into her prime as a dancer, and Riya hoped her friend would get the recognition—and roles—she deserved. Riya wasn't above using her minor magical ability with doors to find opportunities for her honest and hard-working friend.

In time with the music by a modern Native American composer, Riya called out, "Four, five, six!"

The dancers executed Riya's choreography perfectly and continued through the fight sequence. The rock sequence went off without a hitch. Whitney had obviously been practicing with the slingshot as Riya had suggested, because her little foam "rocks" hit Kenji's demon almost every time. They'd developed various choreographic contingencies for missed shots, but it was much better when Whitney nailed her target.

With Kenji's demon vanquished, Whitney's bird woman and Mack's native shaman character twined ever closer with a celebratory dance, ending in a romantic almost-kiss as the music's last, plaintive flute note echoed.

"And fade to black," called Riya. "Perfect. Really great work. We'll figure out your entrance and exit once we're in the theater." She looked at the clock on the wall. "Take ten, but Denise wants us all in the big classroom at a quarter of eight for a big announcement."

Mack made a beeline for the drinking fountain, rotating his right shoulder as he went. He strained it while on his moving-company job about a month ago, and it still bothered him.

Kenji sat on the floor in a full-splits position, then leaned forward to fish his phone out of his backpack to check messages. In addition to dance classes, he taught three very popular yoga classes during the week, and Riya wouldn't be surprised if some of the students paid just for the privilege of seeing him sit like that in shorts. She had to admit she enjoyed the view, too, but she was the wrong gender for Kenji.

Riya closed the music sound file on her computer, then added a couple of notes to her "to do" list. With only five days until opening night, the list was growing like a weed.

Whitney grabbed a bottle of water from her bag and sauntered closer. "Did Denise decide which performance the company's going to video? I want a copy."

"The Saturday matinee," said Riya. "It'll be good to have St. Peters' name on your résumé."

Whitney made a sour face. "Great. I can say 'I was 'tree number two.' It's *your* piece I want for my demo reel. You work with us to tailor the piece to our strengths, rather than get pissy when we can't conform to the piece."

Riya thanked her friend for the compliment, but refrained from commenting on Jonathan St. Peters, the hotshot, special guest choreographer from New York. Not that Riya disagreed with Whitney, but Riya was about to be named as the new artistic director of the company, which meant she needed to practice diplomacy —not her strong suit.

She hoped Denise's big announcement would be about the new position, because the board of directors had kept Riya on hold for the last two months. Riya was already doing the work for free, so it would be nice to have the official title and get paid a living wage, or what passed for it in the nonprofit dance world in Denver, Colorado. At least Maruaway paid a stipend to the dancers. Far too many dance companies paid everyone *but* the dancers, shamelessly taking advantage of their desire to dance and their dreams of being discovered.

"Some of us are hitting the pub around the corner after rehearsal. Want to come?" Whitney was a born social organizer and loved bringing friends together. If Riya ever started a charity, she'd hire Whitney as the outreach director.

"Tempting, but I have the early shift at the coffee house." Riya shut her computer and slid it into her bright orange and purple bag. She was done with her choreography duties for the evening, but she was also a dancer in two other pieces and the big "Spring Awakening" piece by St. Peters, so her night was far from over. "I still need to check in with our sound tech to make sure she has everything she needs."

"Thank God I don't have to be at the bank until nine all this week," said Whitney. "Speaking of jobs, Mack says The Douche got fired again." She shook her head. "How do you fail at being a store greeter? Anyway, he told Mack he's moving back to Chicago, where his *genius*"—she made air quotes—"will be appreciated."

Riya shook her head. "Chicago can have him. I can't believe I fell for his metric ton of bullshit. Author, my ass," said Riya. She slipped into her clogs, then checked to make sure she hadn't left a trail of belongings behind her. "The fact that he called himself 'The Duke,' in the third person, should have been my first clue."

It had hurt to discover her ex-boyfriend, Carl "Duke" Polliard, part-time job-hopper and full-time author of nineteen unfinished manuscripts for the great American novel, had "friends with kinky benefits" arrangements with half the women in town. At least she'd figured it out before letting him move in with her, like he'd wanted.

"I hear you." Whitney slung her bag's strap over her shoulder. "I just need to meet guys who aren't dancers or bankers."

Riya caught up with her friend. "That's why I volunteer at the rehab center. It's hard to feel sorry for yourself when you see what some of the war veterans or accident victims are going through."

She loved using her dance background to help people find new ways of using their bodies so they could regain mobility and self-sufficiency. Too bad she couldn't do that for a living, instead of pouring coffee and taking on freelance choreography gigs. She loved dancing, and couldn't imagine her life without it, but she didn't want it to be her *only* life.

She wanted a home, one she could nest in. Nesting was in her blood, considering the number of bird shifters and bird-like demigods on her mother's side of the family. Her flighty parents moved often and loved to travel, and as a child, she'd logged more air hours than most pilots.

Her cloud spirit father could only visit the Earth dimension for a few months at a time, or he'd start to go misty around the edges. Riya's mother was half human and half avian demigod, and could shift into any bird form she chose. Riya was a rare genetic fluke, mostly human with no shifting ability, or ability to become fog like her cousins could, or ability to see the future like her grandmother could. Outside of her parents, most of her magical family shunned her. At least she healed fast, and she'd lately gotten better at working magic.

And while envisioning her dream nest, she wanted it to include pets, children, and a sexy dream warrior shaman with complex, intricate designs inked on his very lickable skin. She'd dreamed of him most nights for the past month. He talked to her a lot, as if he didn't have anyone else to share his thoughts with, but frustratingly, only saw her as an exotic bird. Riya was afraid her subconscious was comforting her with dreams of an insanely hot, talon-footed man because her real love life was so disappointing.

She set aside her worries as she and Whitney walked into the studio's largest classroom and joined the twelve other dancers who would be performing in the upcoming spring concert. Riya crossed to the long, mirrored wall and set her bag down, then used the waist-high barre to support a series of quick leg and back stretches. She was one of the older dancers in the company, and it paid to treat her thirty-year-old body with respect.

Riya had to give credit to Denise, the company's new executive director. The woman was blithely ignorant about dance production, but she knew how to sell tickets and attract big donors, enough to double the size of the professional company. The publicity blitz had the week-end's performances half sold already, meaning their budget had already broken even. Bringing in Jonathan St. Peters helped. He looked and sounded like a charming, humble, fun guy in all the interviews. Too bad the real man didn't match his public persona.

As if her disgruntled thought conjured him, St. Peters strutted into the room, followed by Denise right after him. She couldn't be dissuaded from walking on their elderly marley dance floor in her spiked heels, despite the "no street shoes allowed" sign at every entrance. Her tailored blue silk business suit flattered her plump figure.

Denise cleared her throat. "I know it's the last rehearsal night before you move into the theater, and you're busy, but I wanted to share two pieces of good news. First, both Saturday performances are already sold out. Sunday is half gone, and opening night only has about twenty seats left."

The dancers clapped and cheered. A full house of close to three hundred added awesome energy to live performances.

"Riya, could you come up front?" Denise smiled.

Riya tried to play it cool as she walked up front, but

she couldn't control the little spring in her step. Finally, her hard work was about to be rewarded.

"The second piece of good news is that we have a new sponsor, the Spencer Emerson Foundation, to underwrite the choreography costs. So, not only do Riya and Jonathan actually get paid"—she paused for the titter of laughter—"but it means we can afford for Jonathan to stay with us all week, through the final performance."

Riya's stomach went sour. Not only was she still in limbo as far as the artistic director position, but she and the other women in the company would have to put up with a full week of Mr. Snooty McGrab-Hands, as Whitney had so eloquently named him, instead of just for opening night. Riya hastily plastered a smile on her face and returned her attention to Denise.

"...foundation representative wants to meet our choreographers tonight at eight. It'll only take a few minutes, but he'd like to put faces to the names." Denise smiled at everyone. "Keep up the good work, everyone, and let's make it a great show." At least they'd convinced her to stop saying "break a leg."

Denise turned to leave, and St. Peters crossed to Julia, a short, big-breasted woman with explosive dance energy. St. Peters hadn't given up trying to talk her into appearing topless for a brief segment in his "Spring Awakening" piece, despite Julia's repeated refusals. Riya had already turned him down flat. She stayed long enough to make sure Julia didn't need support, then followed after Denise, who was headed to her office.

"Denise, do you have a minute?"

"Sure," said Denise. Even in heels, she was shorter than Riya by a good six inches, with artfully colored auburn hair that she wore in styles designed to give her more height. She was always impeccably dressed.

"I was hoping to hear something about the artistic director position you offered. It's been over two months now, and I'm putting in a lot of extra hours."

"I know, and I'm sorry about that." Denise smiled apologetically. "I keep pushing the board because we need that position filled, but they keep getting sidetracked by the crisis of the moment, and they never get to the rest of their agenda. The board chair is a nice man, but he doesn't know how to run a meeting." Her expression said she'd whip them into shape if she were in charge.

Denise took the plastic lid off a small cheese tray. "Getting Jonathan to stay is a lucky break for us. He's great at publicity." She crossed to the credenza and pulled out four wine glasses. "I have big dreams for this company. Maruaway is poised to really make a splash."

The board had hired Denise six months ago because she'd promised to make good use of her New York arts-world contacts. She'd delivered in spades by landing several new big donors and St. Peters. She was working on getting underwriters to bring in an A-list Russian choreographer for the company's annual holiday concert of *Modern Fairy Tales*.

"I hope so," said Riya. She could take or leave being in the spotlight, as long as she got to dance and choreograph, but the rest of the young and talented company deserved their chance to shine. "I'd like to help make that happen."

Denise sidled closer. "Then can I give you a word of advice?" She glanced at the open door, then lowered her voice. "Be *nice* to Jonathan, because he could really help the company. He talks about you all the time, how he'd love to nurture your talent. I think he's very attracted you." Denise smiled and winked. "It's so hard for straight men to get ahead in the dance world."

Riya didn't know whether to be appalled that she was all but being asked to sleep with St. Peters for the good of the company, or to laugh outright at Denise's cluelessness about how little sexual orientation mattered to professional dancers. Talent, integrity, and hard work mattered far more.

"I'll, uhm, keep that in mind," Riya said with a weak smile, then hurriedly changed the subject. "I'm not exactly dressed for a meet-and-greet." She looked down at her threadbare and faded "Mechanoid Rebellion" T-shirt, which only partially hid her screaming yellow sports bra. Her favorite flame-patterned leggings had a hole in one knee. She knew her wavy hair was escaping from the sloppy bun at the back of her head, and its navy-to-turquoise color wasn't exactly corporate.

"You're fine. You look like a working dancer." Riya couldn't tell if that was a compliment or not.

St. Peters arrived just as Denise glanced at her watch. He dressed like an artist's conception of a poet, with black leather pants and high-heeled boots, an off-white puffy-sleeved shirt, belted at the waist, and a long, red silk scarf around his neck. All he needed was long, flowing hair and a pretentious British accent.

Riya turned away for a moment, because he took his style very seriously, and she knew she couldn't keep the amusement off her face. He was handsome, with chiseled features and sparkling blue eyes, and a dancer's tight physique, but his personality killed any possible attraction.

Riya was saved from having to "be nice" by the arrival of the Spencer Emerson Foundation representative, who turned out to be Spencer Emerson himself. He was a distinguished man in his late forties, with a silver hairline beginning to recede at the temples. He and St. Peters were about the same height, only a couple of inches taller than Riya. Emerson was dressed like he was about to step onto the red carpet at the Academy Awards. His Italian shoes alone probably cost more than she made in a month. Who dressed like that on a Monday evening in Denver?

"Spencer Emerson," he said, holding his hand out, his smile wide, almost crocodilian. "You must be the renowned Jonathan St. Peters."

St. Peters grinned, clearly flattered. "It's a pleasure to meet you." He shook Emerson's hand.

Emerson turned to Riya. "Love the hair. And you are?"

She smiled. "Riya Sanobal." She shook his proffered hand and instantly regretted it.

For the few moments their skin was in contact, she felt a flood of nausea, like she was coming down with the flu, and thought she was seeing double.

She snatched her hand back and quickly sat in the farthest chair to shore up the shields that hid her magic. Her minor abilities and not-quite-human nature weren't noticeable except to high adepts, but Emerson seriously creeped her out.

Riya watched Denise subtly flirt with the man while pouring the wine, and St. Peters bask in Emerson's interest in how he came up with such innovative and varied choreography. They didn't seem to think anything was wrong, even though Emerson's smile looked like it was operated with strings. When Emerson asked about her artistic inspirations, she mumbled vapid, beauty-contest platitudes about watching history and nature programs.

"Oh my goodness, look at the time," said Riya, standing quickly. "I really need to get back to rehearsal."

Denise shot her a deeply annoyed glance, but Riya ignored it. If the board couldn't be bothered to make her artistic director, then Riya-the-hired-choreographer didn't feel obliged to suck up to either Emerson or St. Peters.

At close to midnight, Riya was more than ready to climb into whichever was closest, a hot shower or a soft bed. Fortunately, she'd managed to wolf down the sandwich she'd brought, so at least she wasn't hungry, too.

She'd just finished helping pull the cover over the studio piano when Whitney looked toward the door and muttered a curse. "I love you like a sister, Riya, but blood will be spilled if I have to spend another second with Mr. McGrabby." St. Peters stood at the door, hands on his hips, an impatient look on his face.

Riya picked up the two bags at her feet and handed Whitney's to her. "Go on with you, then," she said in a broad Irish accent. "I can't afford the bail." She winked.

Whitney chuckled as she hugged Riya. "I'll have a beer in honor of your sacrifice. See you tomorrow night." She took off toward the alley exit door, apparently deciding she'd rather walk the long way around the block than go near St. Peters again.

Riya couldn't blame her. He had a habit of not-so-accidental inappropriate touching when showing female dancers how he wanted them to move. The only reason he left Riya unmolested is she'd cheated and used a little magic as a deterrent.

She slid the strap of her bag onto her shoulder and gamely marched toward the door where St. Peters stood.

He smiled engagingly. "Come to dinner with me tomorrow night before rehearsal. I'd like to talk about us collaborating on a piece that would really blow Spencer Emerson's mind."

She just barely stopped herself from saying she'd rather scrub the women's restroom with her personal toothbrush. "It's a kind offer, but I'll be coming straight from work to the theater at five-thirty so we can start haul-in for the sets and costumes."

Her work tomorrow consisted of a free consultation at the rehab center, but she'd be damned if she'd stand up a wounded veteran for the dubious honor of dinner with St. Peters.

He was undaunted. "How about right now? My hotel is only a mile away. We could start with a drink in the bar." He touched her upper arm. Her little spell zapped him, and he pulled away fast. "Damn static electricity."

Riya smiled sympathetically. "The dry Denver climate does that." She managed to turn the lights off and slip past him into the hallway before he could block her. She started toward the front door. He lengthened his stride to keep up.

"Would you please stop walking and look at me for a

minute?" He sounded sincere, almost pleading. Surprised, she did as he asked.

He shoved his hands in the pockets of his leather coat. "I'm going to lay my heart on the line here. Ever since I got here, you've intrigued me, driven me crazy, inspired my dreams. Made me want you." He edged closer. "Exotic ethnic looks like yours are hot right now. You've got more talent than the entire company combined, and you don't even know it. You could write your ticket to wherever you wanted to go—New York, San Francisco, Barcelona."

Riya couldn't tell how much of that was real and how much was his best guess on what she wanted to hear. She'd had enough traveling to last a lifetime, and her "ethnic look" wasn't a ticket to dance anywhere but a Bollywood music video. He definitely wanted something from her. She'd like to ignore him, but if he did have feelings beyond garden-variety lust, she couldn't be that cruel. "I'm flattered, but we don't really know one another." She shook her head. "To be perfectly frank, you've been a jerk."

He rocked back on his heels and stared at the floor instead of meeting her gaze. "I'm sorry. It's a defense mechanism. I feel very vulnerable around you, and I don't know where I stand, so I..." He shrugged a shoulder.

"Push before you're shoved?" she suggested. It didn't explain why he was rude to the others, but she was willing to cut him some slack if it would make it easier on rest of the company.

"I guess." He looked up at her. "Come to dinner, and let me show you the real me. If not tomorrow, how about Wednesday?"

Riya sighed. "Maybe." She held up her hand to forestall his response. "No promises. They don't call final tech and dress rehearsals 'hell week' for nothing." She started walking again. "Let's see how tomorrow goes." She gave him a weary smile. "I'm too tired tonight to do anything but go home."

He beamed. "I'll walk you to your car."

4

S NUG IN HER little apartment bedroom, after a quick, hot shower and time to think, Riya decided she might be to blame for some of St. Peters' attitude. His towering ego reminded her too much of her ex-boyfriend, and he even looked a bit like him, though in much better shape. The Douche would have needed a shoehorn and a jar of lube to get his pudgy thighs and belly into leather pants.

She also resented that the company was paying St. Peters five times what they were paying her, even though she'd choreographed two new pieces, plus selected and rehearsed the set pieces the core company already knew. Not to mention, hired technical staff and managed budgets as the unpaid artistic director. She'd tried to keep her dissatisfaction to herself, but she may not have been as successful as she'd thought.

On the other hand, she had no interest in him as a man. Not a single hormone stirred when he was close, and his smell was about as interesting as lettuce.

She pulled on her nightshirt and turned out the bedside light as she slid between the sheets.

She never realized how important scent was to her until she'd had that remarkably vivid dream a month ago, where the warrior shaman her subconscious had conjured up had smelled of pine, horses, and delicious man. From that day on, she knew she could never settle for anything less in a lover. Which meant she was probably doomed to a solitary life.

She'd had other dreams before and since, but they were instantly forgotten. She remembered each and every one of the dreams with the shaman, the first one most of all.

It had been late one evening, in her studio. She'd made an urban nest out of a converted warehouse, with her own private dance space on the main floor and her living quarters upstairs in what was once the office. For the dance company's spring concert, she'd found an evocative, modern Native American composition that spoke to her, and after securing permission, had begun choreographing to it. She'd gotten stuck about halfway through and couldn't come up with the right movements to match the mixed meter or how the music made her feel. She'd danced herself into frustrated exhaustion, and tried to use her magic to open a door for herself, the way she did with other dancers, or the amputees and injured people she worked with at the rehab center. It hadn't worked, and she'd fallen asleep on her narrow downstairs couch.

She'd awakened to a twilight world, where the colors were both saturated and muted, and the ground was both soft and unforgiving under her bare feet. The sky was unreal and yet familiar, as if she was looking through the back side of a fire opal, all red and blue and gray clouds and full of unfamiliar stars.

The wind blew chilly, and she wished she'd brought her long, fluffy sweater, only to realize that she was already wearing it. She wiggled her toes and watched red jazz oxfords close over them, to go with black-and-red checked leggings she'd worn in the Christmas dance concert. To her delight, the turquoise ends of her hair were decorated with a variety of long, thin brown, turquoise, and red feathers. Her mother would be so pleased that something of her avian heritage was finally visible.

She would have continued playing with her wardrobe if she hadn't heard the sounds of a fight and gone to investigate, as one did in dreams, even though some part of her rational brain said it would be smarter to run away.

The flat scrub desert morphed into an uphill climb with red, rocky outcrops, a surrealistic interpretation of the Native American Puebloan country of the Southwest. She slowly, carefully climbed a stack of rounded red rocks. She flattened herself on top, then inched forward until she could just see over the edge.

Two creatures, knee deep in mist, fought with serious, deadly intent. One was so far from being human that it hurt to look at. It moved in ways that shouldn't be possible. Deep, sickly green with orange splotches, its head and neck arose from the center of its chest. It had two dinosaur-huge legs with three-toed claws and a spiked tail, and two triple-jointed overhead appendages that looked too thin to deliver the powerful blows it was raining on its opponent.

The other creature was much easier on the eyes, and riveted her attention. He looked Native American, with a dark braid of hair on one side of his head. The other side was bare, except for the stunning, detailed, multicolored tattoo that she'd have liked to get a better look at. It seemed to be constantly changing, like the cloud pictures her father used to create for her amusement as a child.

The intricate designs trailed down his neck to his torso and the side of his left arm. He wore a short, beaded loincloth with a thin strap around his hips to keep it in place. She couldn't see much of the front, but from the back, it showcased his beautifully rounded, very worthy ass. From the top of his thighs down, white and brown eagle feathers covered his legs, which ended in sharp, five-toed talons. He had an arrhythmic but graceful gait. Everywhere he stepped, the mist cleared.

The compellingly attractive man was fast and agile, which was a good thing because the ugly green creature, which she decided was a demon, was about a foot taller and fought dirty, pinching, gouging, and spitting. Fortunately, the man had magic at his disposal. When the demon threw a handful of red dust at the bird-legged man's eyes, the man spoke a few unrecognizable words that turned the dust into a cloud of gnats that swarmed the demon's face.

The demon stumbled and spat out words that caused the gnats to burn like tiny fireworks. "Why is your female here, shaman?" Its voice was high and thin. "Can't best me by yourself?" The demon circled to the left, and the shaman countered.

"She's your illusion, fear-maker," said the shaman. She knew they were talking about her, but all she could think about was how sexy his voice sounded, deep and resonant.

"I don't make fear," snarled the demon, clearly affronted.

"Then what are these?" The shaman made a sweeping gesture, and mist cleared behind the demon. Three upright windows appeared, resting on the ground, each with a different look and style, like examples in an architectural catalog. One was sleek and modern, one had desert camouflage netting for curtains, and the third was covered with brown paper, as if about to be painted.

"I didn't *make* them." The demon sounded like a politician parsing the truth.

"No, but you gave them the materials. That's against the treaty." The shaman's tone was unyielding. "As all from your realm know."

The demon reversed course and circled right, and again the shaman countered. Without warning, the demon's spiked tail made a vicious strike that impaled the shaman's left lower leg. It didn't seem to hurt him, but it restricted the shaman's movements. The demon rained down blows against the shaman that he couldn't duck.

It made Riya mad, like when she was a child, and bullies ganged up on a younger kid. If she had her favorite slingshot and some nice stones, she'd show the blotchy green demon a thing or two. Suddenly, she felt a weight in her hand, and there was the slingshot she'd made in Dublin when she was eleven, and her other hand held perfect-sized, oval stones. She grinned. Her dream magic was even better than a teleportation device from a science fiction show.

She took aim and waited for her shot, then nailed the

demon right on what looked like its nose. It roared and arched back, a yellow ichor flowing freely. The spiked tail jerked free of the shaman's leg, but the movement pulled him off his taloned feet. Riya shot three more stones as fast as she could, to keep the demon off balance until the shaman could scramble up again. The rocks had more impact than she would have expected.

The shaman's feathered leg had a hole in it that didn't bleed. Riya's dream self realized it must be a prosthesis, like the veterans she'd seen at the rehab center, which also explained his syncopated gait.

The demon made one last assault, but the shaman's skill and a couple more of her well-aimed rocks drove it to its knees in submission.

"Banish me, then, Warrior," said the demon. Despite the newly nasal tone, it sounded resigned to its fate, almost despairing.

"What say you, Woman of the Rocks?" The shaman's voice was loud enough to echo off the rest of the rock walls that were revealed when the mist faded.

There was no point in staying hidden anymore, so she jumped down onto the rust-colored ground with an impossible-in-real-life, somersaulting leap. Unfortunately, the shaman was focused on the demon and didn't see her stick the landing like a champion gymnast. "What do I say about what?"

"Shall this *kaga* be banished to..." The shaman glanced at her, then did a double take, his eyes riveted on her. "What *are* you?"

She looked down and realized that while she'd been concentrating on the fight, her subconscious had dressed her in the East Indian-style costume she'd worn for a piece last summer's dance concert, about a Hindu warrior goddess who defeated demons. "Just a dancer from the Mile High City." She shimmied her hips to make the bells sound and stomped her feet to create a rhythmic phrase.

She was liking this dream. She was really liking the shaman's plainly avid interest in her body, because his was drawing hers like a lodestone. She had to fight not to move closer to him, even though the spike-tailed demon was still a threat.

The shaman licked his lips, making her wish she could do that for him to find out what he tasted like. She never allowed herself those kinds of thoughts in real life, but in her delightfully lucid dream, it felt good to allow her lascivious fantasies free rein.

He cleared his throat. "Shall the *kaga* be banished to its realm of origin?"

Her sexy fantasy dream had gotten politically weighty all of a sudden. "Is deportation the usual punishment for breaking the law?" She frowned. "Do ugly, no-ass demons even have rights here?"

A smile twitched across his mouth. "It's open to interpretation."

Riya shrugged. "Since it's my dream, then, I say let it off with a warning." She put her fists on her hips and glared at the demon. "Don't do whatever bad thing you did with those window thingies again, or the hot, sexy warrior will kick your sorry excuse for an ass back to, uh, the zombie zone."

She materialized an oversized red bandanna into her hand and lobbed it toward the demon. A puzzled expression crossed its surprisingly humanoid face, if she discounted the whole head-growing-out-of-the-chest thing. "For your bloody nose," she said. The yellow ichor still streamed from it, dripping steadily into the absorbent red dust. "Assuming that *is* your nose, and not some body part I don't want to know about."

The shaman said something in a Native American-sounding language. The demon nodded and picked up the bandanna, then rose to its clawed feet. "I am called Moth Dust. I acknowledge the debt." It carefully folded the bandanna and slipped it under a flap of skin on its belly she hadn't noticed until then. With a mighty leap, it bounded away like a disturbing kangaroo.

She shook her head in amazement. "Its name is Moth Dust?"

"Demons have inexplicable ideas about public names." Even as he spoke, her feet started walking her toward the shaman. She was relieved to see that he was walking toward her as well. His fascinating tattoo was almost alive, like watching a plasma cloud, and his strength was palpable. "What about your leg?" She pointed to the through-and-through hole where the demon's tail spike had impaled it. "Can it be fixed?"

"Yes, with a little magic." He pointed to the slingshot still in her hand. "Where did you learn to shoot like that?"

"Secondary school in Ireland." Her eyes traced the tattoos down his body, noting they skirted his brown nipple and curled onto the sculpted ridges of his abdominal muscles and down his hip. "Are you really a warrior?"

"Yes. What are you doing here in dreamwalk?"

"Enjoying the view," she said honestly. She stopped about three feet away from him and smiled, pleased that he was five or six inches taller than she was. "You're outrageously sexy. This is the best dream ever. I should try lucid dreaming to solve my choreography problems a whole lot more often."

"You're a stunningly attractive woman. Very distracting." He tilted his head. "You think you're dreaming?"

"Well, yeah." She gave him a saucy wink. "I sure as hell wouldn't do this"—she closed the distance between them and put her hands on his shoulders—"if I was awake." She drew in the scent of him. Human male, crushed pine needles, and freshly groomed horses. The feel of his skin under her hands warmed her like they were making an electrical circuit. She could drown in his deep brown eyes. "Or this." She slid her hands to the sides of his face and rose up on her toes to kiss him. After a moment's hesitation, he kissed her back.

It felt so wonderful, and so perfectly right, that she had to do it again, this time with abandon. The taste of him when he sent his tongue into her willing mouth sent a thrill through her body that had her nipples aching and her core clenching.

He moaned, or she did, as his hands glided down her back and onto her hips, where they caressed and kneaded, pulling her close. The feel of his feathered leg on the skin of her thigh was erotic. Her panties dampened. She slipped a hand between their bodies to rub a light thumb over his puffy nipple and felt it pebble. He definitely moaned that time...

...and she awoke on the lumpy couch in her cold studio, breasts tingling and nipples aching to be touched, core pulsing. Whoever set off the car alarm that had awakened her deserved to die.

The clock said twelve midnight. Great. She was a freakin' modern Cinderella.

When she sat up, blearily rubbing her eyes, she hadn't known if she was relieved or disappointed to find out she was still wearing the same old rehearsal sweats she'd been wearing when she'd fallen asleep.

Her subconscious had obviously raided recent and childhood memories for the plot of that vivid and unforgettable dream. In real life, she would never even think of kissing a total stranger and wondering how to get him out of his loincloth, especially not with her abysmal boyfriend track record. But in the dream, with the mouthwateringly sexy, painted shaman, hell yes, and she'd do it again.

Apparently, her subconscious had taken that to heart and created a whole series of dreams about the smoking-hot shaman in the past month. Unfortunately, her annoying imagination decided she had to be some sort of exotic bird creature that followed him around, rather than a human woman who wanted to take up where the kiss left off.

In her dreams, the warrior enjoyed her company and talked to her about things magical and mundane, like the fact that the fear-eater demon they'd defeated occupied a useful niche in the "dreamwalk." Or the fact that he was rightfully called a medicine man, and the only one left in his tribe who could dreamwalk. Or the fact that he missed his grandfather, who'd recently died.

She'd spoken to him with words, but all he apparently heard was birdsong. She had no idea what her subconscious meant by that, other than her desire to please her mother by finding her bird form at last, or that men and women didn't communicate as well as they should. Her subconscious apparently had an idea file full of clichés.

One good thing came of the dreams. The fight with the demon had provided the ideal storyline for her choreography, and she'd snagged the perfect company dancers for the roles. The dreamwalk had looked like magical realism to her, and that's what she'd worked with the dancers and costumer to achieve. She loved the piece and hoped the audiences would, too.

Which brought her back to the immediate problem of what to do about Jonathan St. Peters. She stared up at the reflected moonlight on her darkened ceiling, knowing she should be sleeping, but her brain was unwilling to shut down yet. No real, live man could match her dream warrior, but she knew she could do better than St. Peters.

She owed him the courtesy of a professional relationship, but after only a few weeks' worth of dreamy nights with her medicine man, a whole year's worth of days with St. Peters wasn't going to change her feelings. When he'd tried to kiss her cheek before he let her get in her car, the squick factor of having his lips anywhere on her made her evade him like a mixed martial arts fighter ducking a strike. And no matter what Denise suggested, it wasn't right to let St. Peters believe that Riya's feelings would change.

As she finally drifted off to sleep, she hoped her subconscious would send her to the warrior again, to distract her from her melancholy musings.

$\mathbf{\mathscr{L}}$ *5* $\mathbf{\mathscr{K}}$

I DRIÁN EASED HIMSELF carefully into the last row of main floor seats of the Wilhelmina Dryer Theatre. His magic hid him in the semi-darkness, unless someone knew how to look, but he didn't want to make more noise than necessary. The audience seating sections were shallow, only fifteen rows deep, but very wide, with four aisles, to accommodate the equally wide stage. The wispy ghosts of the factory workers said it had been built in the twenties as a shoe manufacturing plant. They liked show business.

The drive north to Denver had been easy enough, once he'd hit I-25. Over the years, he and his grandfather had magically tinkered with the truck to make it fast and invisible to police radar, so he'd only had to stop for food, bathrooms, and to stretch his right leg. The brace was still rubbing hard in one spot. Once in Denver, a stop at a coffee shop with free internet gave him the names of dance companies and schools to try.

It has taken the rest of the day and a couple of spells to

track down a turquoise-haired choreographer and the place where she'd be that evening. He'd used a little earth magic to slip into the theater unseen and conceal himself in the audience area to wait.

Black Fox offered to scout around, and Idrián gratefully agreed, looking forward to a brief respite from his company. He loved his grandfather, but his new spirit form gave him the freedom to pop in and out without warning, and he was as opinionated as ever.

Idrián was just in time to see part of a rehearsal on the stage, where a blond man, whose name was apparently St. Peters, was capturing video of it using his tablet. To Idrián's untutored eye, the three dancers' movements looked intriguing, and he wished he could have seen the rest of it. He recognized the music they were using immediately—his cousin Román had composed it.

The dancers left, and St. Peters kneeled down on the front of the stage, tapping on the tablet rapidly. When he was finished, he closed the tablet's cover and slipped it into a messenger bag on the floor, then pulled out a phone and stood while he made a call. He was in good shape and carried himself with the confident ease of an athlete. He was handsome enough to be a model, and dressed like it, too—a blue velvet shirt and sleek leather pants with a low-slung belt.

"I just sent it," St. Peters said. The theater's acoustics were good enough for Idrián to hear him easily. "Tell me what you think." He listened for a long moment, nodding, his smile growing with each second. "Thank you." He grinned and gave a fist-pump gesture.

Idrián was suddenly distracted by the feel of a slight breeze that became a blaze of tingles dancing across his skin. He looked to his left and saw a woman entering from the swinging doors that led to the lobby, about twelve feet from where he sat.

She was using a low-power spell to make most people look somewhere else besides at her, but the magnetism of her physical presence made it hard for him to look at anything *but* her. He didn't need his grandfather's ghostly whispering to tell him that she was the woman from dreamwalk, with her shaded turquoise hair, beautiful face with wide mouth and large brown eyes, and curvaceously sculpted body. Her wildly patterned leggings hugged her legs like a second skin, and the unzipped black hoodie she wore gaped open to show a tight, red crop-top that contained her lush, full breasts.

Dreamwalk was the dream version of the world, and reality often didn't match it, but in this case, the woman in real life beat the dreamwalk version, hands down. The scent of her, feathers and tangerine and incense, hit him squarely in the chest and traveled instantly to his groin, making the front of his jeans suddenly too tight. He barely stopped himself from standing up to get closer.

The oblivious blond man on stage was focused on his call. "No, no, she only did the rehearsing for *Red Dust Warrior*. The choreography is all mine. I only let them put her name on it in the program because I felt sorry for her. They'd already selected the music, and she really tried, but…" His voice sounded regretful, but it was belied by a huge grin as he listened. "Exactly, Mr. Emerson. I love nurturing talent wherever I find it. It's so rewarding."

The rising anger from the woman near him was like static electricity shocks on Idrián's sensitive scarred skin. She stalked quickly down the aisle, shoulder bag thumping against her hip. She gestured, and both doors of the loading dock slammed closed like a gunshot.

St. Peters jumped and fumbled his phone, but caught it. He looked at the doors, then turned toward the right wing. "Sorry, the wind blew a door shut." After another long pause, he said, "Yes, that works for me. Look, I'd better let you go. I have a lot to do tonight to get this performance in shape. Regional companies can be so clueless."

As St. Peters was finishing his conversation, Riya approached the stage and quietly walked up the stairs on the left side. Idrián felt it in his chest when she dropped her "don't look" spell. She stood with her legs apart, arms crossed, staring at St. Peters as he finished his conversation.

"You, too, Spencer." The blond man pressed a button on his phone and slid it in his pocket. The woman cleared her throat. The blond man whirled around, then stepped back, clearly startled. "Good God, Riya, you scared the life out of me!"

"Tempting," she said bitingly. "Care to explain why you told Spencer Emerson you choreographed *Red Dust Warrior*?"

"It's not what you think." He smoothed back the hair that had fallen in front of his face. "I did it for you. For the company." He spread his arms wide. "Mr. Emerson was going to pull his foundation's funding because he thought the company lied about how much I was involved in the program. You wouldn't have gotten paid, otherwise."

Riya looked nonplussed. "I don't know what—"

"What are you doing here so early?" His interruption was laced with accusation. "I thought you'd be at work."

"When you insisted the dancers be here early because you needed to fix things in *my* piece, Whitney called me." Her tone took on a sharp edge. "The message to me must have gone astray."

"Must have. It's my job to make this program the best it can be, sweetheart." He gave her an indulgent smile. "Denise asked me to look at all the pieces, as the new artistic director."

Idrián felt an irrational stab of jealousy at St. Peters' endearment for her. *That's your dick talking*, he admonished himself, but it didn't help.

Riya whipped a phone out of a pocket in her hoodie and used one hand to dial. She put it on speaker, so they all heard when the call was answered.

"Maruaway Dance Theater, Denise speaking." The sound was tinny but audible.

"Hi, it's Riya and Jonathan St. Peters on speaker. He says he's the new artistic director. Is that true?"

The woman on the phone was silent. Riya's face paled.

Idrián wanted to kill whoever it was on the phone, right after he killed St. Peters, whose pretend-sympathetic look wouldn't fool a blind man.

Black Fox waved a spectral hand like a strobe in front of Idrián's face. "Time to go."

"What?" whispered Idrián, bobbing his head so he could keep watching Riya.

Black Fox floated so his face was in front of Idrián's. "You're slow. You have to be ready to catch her. She'll be leaving soon."

Idrián glared at Black Fox. "How do you know that?"

"I'm an expert in mad women. Up."

Idrián knew he'd get no peace until he complied. Besides, Black Fox did know mad women, because he was usually the one making them mad. Idrián grabbed his cane and levered himself to his feet in the narrow space.

Down on the stage, the woman on the phone said, *"It's a temporary appointment, for the summer. I... that is, the board and I felt you needed a mentor, someone more experienced in sponsor relations. I was going to talk to you about it after open... er, tomorrow."*

"How very thoughtful of you." The acid in Riya's tone could etch titanium. St. Peters winced.

"You're obviously upset. I have an important meeting tonight, but we can talk about this tomorrow."

Idrián sidestepped along the row and eased himself carefully into the aisle. He was uncomfortable with how deeply angry he was on Riya's behalf. He didn't even know her, and his recent experience proved he was a rotten judge of women.

"Lobby," hissed his grandfather, making shooing motions at him like he was one of the ranch's goats.

On the stage, Riya's voice was full of dire promise. "Oh, yes, we *will* talk tomorrow." She pressed a button on her phone, then slid it back into her pocket.

St. Peters held up his hands. "It was all Denise's idea."

Idrián turned and limped up the slight incline toward the lobby doors. His back and legs were stiff with tension.

"Liar." She packed an amazing amount of disdain into that short word.

"Now, sweetheart, let's calm—"

"Stop right there. First, only my boyfriend calls me sweetheart. Second, if you don't tell Spencer Emerson who really choreographed *Red Dust Warrior*, my mother's very expensive lawyers will enjoy reaming you for every cent you've got. Third, if you changed even a single…"

Idrián pushed through the swinging door as quickly as he could.

With the lobby door closed, Idrián could hear no more. It was just as well. He needed time to calm down, because he'd learned the hard way during rehabilitation that rage and walking didn't mix.

He stepped closer to the front of the lobby and let his invisibility magic slip away. The box office staff didn't notice him. He looked south out the wide front windows to the sunny blue sky, and took several deep, calming breaths. He still wanted to punch the people who were mistreating Riya, but he was no longer contemplating using his earth magic to bury them in the rubble of the theater. It disconcerted him that his former girlfriend hadn't generated anything like the depth of feeling caused by his dreamwalk woman. Even if she wasn't his, and might never be.

Black Fox popped into view in front of Idrián, then pointed to about ten feet in front of the swinging doors. "Go stand there, Eaglefoot, so she can't miss you."

When Black Fox used Idrián's family-only nickname, it usually meant he wanted something, but Idrián sighed and did as his grandfather asked. He momentarily wished for the magic to make himself look whole again, but it was a bad idea. He could never trust that she'd—

The doors burst open with a bang, and Riya exploded through them, half turned toward the theater, yelling, "And *never* would be too soon to see you again!"

Idrián tried to move out of her way, but he misjudged

his step, which put him directly in her path as she spun around. Her momentum propelled her straight into him, and they tumbled down in a forward flurry of arms and legs. He barely had time to twist so that her head banged his chest instead of the carpeted floor, but he couldn't keep her hip from colliding with his leg brace. They rolled to a stop and stayed together, body to body, for a heart-stopping, electrifying moment.

❦ 6 ❦

RIYA WAS SO overwhelmed she nearly burst into tears. "Oh my God, I'm so sorry." She'd been so outraged that she'd nearly revealed her magic to zap that slime, St. Peters, just to wipe the smug smile off his face, and then, when making her overly dramatic—but very satisfying—grand exit, she'd smashed into an old man with a cane.

Except he wasn't an old man, he was a dark-eyed, hard-bodied man with burn scars on his face and whose touch set her body tingling in ways that she'd never felt and wanted more of. Embarrassed, she pushed up to her hands and knees. "Are you okay?"

The man blinked once. "Yes, I seem to be. What about you?" A hint of a Spanish accent colored his consonants.

"I'm fine, thanks to you being my cushion." She scrambled to her feet and stepped back. His left leg was bent at an impossible angle, and she panicked until she realized it was a prosthesis that had come loose in their fall. "How can I help you?" She'd learned from her volunteer sessions in rehab that each person had his or her own way of recovering, and offering help was much better than interfering with his process.

As the dark-haired man sat up, his long hair drifted forward, and his western-style shirt gaped open where the front snaps had come undone. The burn scars didn't disguise his beautifully muscled, very masculine chest. Riya flushed to realize she was blatantly ogling him and tried to keep her eyes on his face as he snapped his shirt closed. He was clearly Native American, and ruggedly handsome, with a wide, generous mouth. His imposing, slightly crooked nose gave his face character. His eyes were deep brown, almost black, with long lashes. He was also a magic user of some sort, but she couldn't tell what kind.

"Your bag is on my foot," he said.

"What?" She looked where he was pointing. Her bag was evidently the reason his prosthesis had come loose. She scooped up the offending bag and held it close to her chest. "Sorry."

"No harm done." He rolled up the loose leg of his jeans and, leaning forward, held his prosthetic leg still while he pushed his sock-wrapped stump into it. The prosthesis was a style she'd never seen before, with no connecting pin, and a wire-form lower leg with an elegant, ornately articulated ankle. The athletic shoe encasing its foot looked prosaic by comparison. With the help of his cane, he got to his feet, then bounced on the leg a couple of times to seat his stump in the prosthesis.

He gave her a lopsided smile. "I'm Idrián Odair." His name sounded Spanish, with the accent on the last syllable.

"Riya Sanobal." Her wayward sense of humor got the better of her. "Nice to run into you." She stuck her hand out.

His smile widened as he shook her hand. "Unforgettable."

For as long as their skin touched, she felt deliciously energized, the exact opposite of when she'd had to shake hands with the creepy Spencer Emerson the night before. Which reminded her of the last twenty-four hours, and threatened to send her thoughts down dark paths.

Impulsively, she asked, "Could I make up for my carelessness by treating you to an early dinner?" She glanced back toward the theater, then to the intriguing man in front of her. "I'm taking the whole evening off, since the new artistic director is here to *save* us." She didn't bother to keep the sarcasm from her tone. An hour or two with Idrián was much more appealing than spending another infuriating second anywhere near St. Peters. She wouldn't be good for anyone's morale that night, and as for St. Peters, the theater owners took a dim view of real blood on their stage.

Idrián was frowning at something to the right of her, but he quickly looked back to her. "Are you sure your boyfriend won't mind? The one who calls you 'sweetheart'?"

She was puzzled for a moment, then remembered what she'd yelled at St. Peters. It must have been loud enough to hear in the lobby. "Pfft." She waved a dismissive hand. "I haven't had a boyfriend in months. I just wanted St. Peters to leave me alone." She gave him a crooked smile. "So, dinner?"

He nodded. "Yes, if we each pay." He flicked his eyes at

the same place to her right again. "The spot I was standing in made me impossible to miss."

He agreed to follow her to a diner in her neighborhood. As luck would have it, she'd parked her little SUV right next to his truck.

Something about the way he walked gave her a strong sense of *déjà vu*, but she didn't know why. His injuries were memorable, but they didn't bother her, and she liked that he'd owned his burn scar by adding a stylized eagle on his skull. With her dance-as-rehab work, she'd long ago learned to look past what a body looked like, regardless of how damaged—or pretty—to see the person inside. She'd let herself forget that lesson with her six-timing ex-boyfriend because she'd been lonely, and with the thieving St. Peters, because she'd wanted to help the company. Never again, she vowed.

She watched as he unlocked the door to his once-white, seen-many-better-days truck, to make sure he wasn't suffering ill effects from their collision. The New Mexico license plate triggered a warm memory of red desert and rocks, and realization suddenly dawned on her. "You're the Red Dust Warrior."

He looked at her, eyebrows raised. "I'm the what?"

She flushed. "Sorry, don't mind me. I'm just a dancer." She twirled a finger at her temple to indicate she was loony. It was what most people thought of artists.

"Tell me," he said gently. "I won't laugh."

"I had a dream about you about a month ago. You had talons for feet. We fought a demon." There, she'd said it. Now he could slowly back away from the crazy woman.

A corner of his mouth twitched in a smile. "I had the same dream."

She laughed. "You did not." She appreciated that he was trying to humor her.

"I did." He took a step closer. "You had a slingshot." He touched his fingers to his lips. "You kissed me. Twice."

And now all she could focus on was his mouth, wondering if he tasted the same in real life. She licked her lips.

"I've been looking for you ever since."

That startled her. "You have? But I've seen you almost every... Oh, you mean here, in real life." That was even more startling. "Why?"

"Because you're a dreamwalker..." His words trailed off as he stared at her a moment. His eyes widened. "You're the bird with the long turquoise feathers and a song like bells." He sighed, as if disgusted with himself. "You've been there all along."

She glanced at the busy street. "Look, I don't want to seem pushy, but I think we need to talk, and not in public." Her intuition said he could be trusted, and her body was definitely in favor of anything that got her alone with him. "We could go to my place. It's protected, and I know the best takeout restaurants in town."

"Yes, we do need to talk." Inexplicably, he winced and put a hand over his left ear.

Over dinner, he told her about his National Guard service in the tank division and the bomb that had ended his career, about his sand painting commercial art, and about his ranch, which he clearly loved and said was better physical therapy than anything the VA offered.

When he mentioned it was near Magic, New Mexico, she told him her mother had always told her it would be a safe place to go in an emergency. She described her own mixed-up ancestry and mostly human nature, her choice of a dance career over formal magic study, her years of dancing and choreographing movement theatre in Europe and the U.S., and her unconventional volunteer work at the rehab center for special cases.

She tossed the empty sandwich wrappers and brought him the glass of water he'd asked for, then sat on the other end of the couch facing him, her legs folded under her.

"So, how did I get to dreamwalk to meet you?"

He'd already explained to her about the dreamwalk plane that was the space between the real world and demon dimensions and other realities, and that access to it manifested differently to individuals who had the dreamwalk gift, which she apparently did. He was an earth mage, with an affinity to his ancestral lands, so to him, it felt like sinking into the soil. For his recently deceased grandfather, a powerful weather mage, it had been like being blown in by a high wind.

"Do you believe in spirits?"

She blinked at the change in subject. "Well, I'd better, or I'd never be able to see my dad again. Pure cloud spirits need the power of belief to be seen in this world. What's that got to do with dreamwalk?"

Idrián looked relieved. "Black Fox—my grandfather—recently transitioned to spirit form. He's here now, and says your portal magic gets you into dreamwalk."

She'd never put a name to her ability, but the name felt right. "He's been talking to you a lot tonight, hasn't he?"

She gave him a teasing smile. "I'm glad to know it's not just voices in your head."

He smiled and nodded, then grew serious. "It's the duty and privilege for dreamwalkers to train others with the talent, and you're the first I've run into. It's very rare for someone untrained to get into dreamwalk without a guide. You need to know how to control your visits, and how to be safe. You've been lucky so far, but you're vulnerable without knowledge."

"Okay, so how do I learn?"

He reached out to her and offered his hand. "We dreamwalk."

She put her hand in his, and took a moment to re-adjust to the thrill of his touch. A flickering image behind the couch caught her eye. She nodded respectfully and focused on him. "Black Fox, I presume?"

"Yes." The old man's ghost stabilized. He wore jeans, a western-style plaid shirt, and a worked silver and turquoise necklace. His white hair was parted in the center, with long braids. The resemblance to Idrián was strong. "Teach Eaglefoot here how to dance." Black Fox winked, then dissolved like ghostly rain.

Idrián sighed. "Don't mind him. He's like a kid in a candy store with his new abilities, popping in and out whenever he feels like it, creating cheesy special effects."

"What's he talking about?"

"I was taught to access my magic through sacred dances." He lifted his right leg with the brace, and patted his left thigh above the prosthesis. "I can't do them anymore."

She recognized the sadness and anger in his voice, like she'd heard from patients at the rehab clinic. "Does it have to be the exact movements? Or is it the rest of it, the part that happens between the steps?"

He looked thoughtful. "I don't know," he finally said. "I always assumed the dance had to be exact."

"When I work with veterans like you in the rehab center, we focus on the outcome, the objective. If you'll let me, I think I can help you find a new door to get there. But not tonight." She squeezed his hand gently. "How do we get to dreamwalk?"

It turned out to be both simpler and harder than she imagined to visit dreamwalk while awake. When he guided her, it was just as easy as opening a door, which she imagined as a sliding-glass door into early summer, her favorite time of year. When he didn't help her, the door wavered like a rippled pond, and she had to struggle to visualize it as being connected to anything. Finally, she hit on the idea of giving herself a steady count in her head, like when she was first learning a new dance, and tuning out all other thoughts besides the feel of the rhythm in her bones and the summer door.

Idrián, tattooed, eagle footed, and gorgeously half-naked in his loincloth, was waiting. "You did well."

"I don't know about that, but I'll get better," she said. "Are you seeing me as a bird or a woman?"

He smiled and eyed her with avid interest, lingering on her hips. "Very much a woman." Her hips were wide, even for a theatrical dancer, but she liked her shape, and was glad he did, too.

"Excellent." In real life, she'd have probably blushed, but in her waking dream, she wanted his admiration. She morphed her "Pluto: Never Forget" T-shirt and yoga pants into a dark blue sari with silver thread, over a golden brown choli top, to complement the turquoise, black, and red accent feathers that intermingled with her hair. She added bells at her hips and wrists and shimmied her hips. "I could do this all day." She grinned at him in delight.

He smiled and held out his hand. "Let me show you dreamwalk."

Just like in real life, the moment she took his hand, power danced under her skin. "Do you feel that, when we touch? It's like we complete a circuit."

He nodded. "It's because we're compatible as dreamwalk partners. We make each other stronger." He smiled wryly. "At least, that's what Black Fox says."

She looked around, but she could only see red ground and clumps of low-growing sage. "Is he here?"

"No. Spirits pass into their own plane. It doesn't intersect with this one, though spirits can look. You could only see him in the real world because you were touching my skin." He tugged her gently. "Come with me."

They started walking together, hand in hand, but it was like walking in a dream, with the environment changing impossibly fast as their feet seemed to skim the ground. His unique gait seemed perfectly natural for taloned feet. Her axis began to tilt, like she'd had several glasses of champagne on an empty stomach.

"You have the nicest butt I've ever seen. Way better than Mack's. He's playing you in my dance. You should wear a loincloth all the time. Although maybe not in the winter." She frowned. "Sorry. I seem to have no filter at the moment."

He laughed. "I forgot to warn you about dreamwalk travel. It loosens whatever anchors you have."

"Let's just pretend I'm three sheets to the wind, okay?" The landscape changed at a dizzying pace, so she concentrated on the fascinating tattoos on his chest, arm, neck, and face that looked like they were illustrating a story, if only she could tell where it started. "This never happened when I was following you around as a bird." Her knees felt wobbly. "Maybe I can learn to shift in dreamwalk. Mumsie would be so proud. Can shifters visit dreamwalk so she can see me?"

Idrián finally stopped and turned to face her. "Riya, look at me." He caught her other hand in his and brought them both to his chest.

The crazily spinning horizon and choppy skies settled down, and the dizzy-drunk feeling evaporated. She blinked a couple of times, then focused on his eagle-gold eyes and took a long, deep, centering breath. "Wow." She grinned. "That was wild." Perhaps it was just as well her wardrobe trick didn't work on him, or he'd have been bare-ass naked the entire trip.

"My fault," he said. "I took you too fast for a beginner." He released one of her hands and cupped the side of her face in his palm, his expression focused and intense. "You are so beautiful."

She tilted her face into his hand and swayed toward him, suddenly drowning in need for him. He groaned, then swooped in and kissed her.

Desire sent her blood racing as she opened her mouth and met his tongue with her own. She clung to him like a life raft for a long moment, reveling in the taste of him. His hands glided down to her bare sides, then back and down. She gasped and tilted her head back when he pulled her hips firmly to his groin, where she felt his promising erection against her abdomen. She undulated her stomach muscles to tease him. His ragged breath near her ear sent shivers through her, and she ground her taut, aching nipples into his chest. He felt so freaking good.

"Riya," he breathed. "We should slow down."

The words slowly penetrated her sensation-swamped brain. "This is bad?"

"Not bad, just..." He caught her wrist before her questing hand could find out if he wore anything under the loincloth. "...unwise."

He knew more about the dreamwalk than she did, so she had to trust him, but her body was definitely *not* on board. It almost hurt to lose contact with his chest. "Like, finger-in-a-light-socket unwise?" She reluctantly pulled her wrist free of his encircling fingers so she could step back. "Or cosign-a-loan-for-your-cousin unwise?"

His mouth twitched with amusement. "More like, what-the-hell-was-in-that-drink unwise." His never-still tattoos glowed more brilliantly where her hand rested on his muscular shoulder. "Dreamwalk makes it too easy to do something we're not ready for in the real world."

He took a small step back, and she let her hand slide off him. The fiery passion in her subsided to a manageable level. She still wanted him, and the bulge in his loincloth said he still wanted her, but their physical connection no longer fanned the flames.

It made her ineffably sad that they couldn't have that in the real world. She turned away before he noticed the sudden tears that threatened. "What are all these windows?"

Now that she was looking anywhere but at him, she noticed they were in the middle of a big field of irregularly spaced mounds of varying heights, like ski-slope moguls made of earth. On top of each was a window embedded face down in the earth. They felt inhabited to her, which made no sense, because they looked weathered and dusty.

"Each dreamwalker experiences them differently. I feel them as living rock formations. My cousin, who is a musician, hears them as songs. They're the graves, for lack of a better word, of the dreamwalker warriors, and the medicine men and spider women of my ancestors. Those that are still spirits in the real world have a presence here, but they can't move freely anymore."

"Can you tell which one belongs to which spirit?"

"No, I don't know how. I'm not the medicine man my grandfather was, and there's no one left to teach me." He sighed, and she had to turn and look. His expression was bleak. "We've lost much. My proud, stubborn ancestors waited too late to accept dreamwalk partners from outside the tribe. My cousin and I are the last of this generation. I'm the only warrior left."

She morphed pockets onto her sari skirt and tucked her hands into them, to keep herself from hugging him like she wanted to. Touching would derail her thoughts, and she wanted to learn all she could about Idrián. She suspected he was ordinarily a private person. "What about your parents?"

"My father was a Mexican national who died in a highway accident when I was seven. After my grandmother died, my mother signed custody of me to Black Fox and moved to Phoenix." He crossed his arms and put his hands under his armpits. "It hurt at the time, because I didn't understand. She has magic but no dreamwalk talent. I do, so Black Fox focused on me. So for my mother, in three short years, her husband died, her mother died, and her father abandoned her." He looked down at his taloned feet. "After the VA hospital discharged me, I wrote and told her I didn't blame her for leaving, and still loved her. We talk, now, from time to time."

She wanted to hug a woman she'd never met, and she couldn't stop the tear that dripped down her cheek, even though she wasn't usually a crier. "Does dreamwalk magnify feelings?"

He tilted his head. "Not exactly. Here, there's nothing holding them back. Dreamwalk is our potential, without the limits or the moorings of the real world. It takes practice to stay off the emotional roller coaster."

She pondered that a moment. "Is that what the fear-eater demon we fought wanted? Potential?"

"Close. When people with dreamwalk potential are sleeping, their stronger dreams sometimes manifest here. Warriors are easiest for me to sense. By ancient treaty, fear-eater demons are allowed here to feed on excess fear, and dreamers wake up feeling better. Lazy demons cheat and send nightmares to the dreamers, then feed on the resulting fear."

She snorted derisively. "Like lazy choreographers who steal work from others, which gets the lazy choreographer a hotshot reputation and other people's jobs?"

He smiled crookedly. "Yes, like that."

"Will I have to fight demons?" She shuffled her feet uncomfortably. "I'm not a warrior like you. I'm just a dancer with a knack for doors."

"I don't know. We can ask the non-warrior ancestors."

He frowned. "Speaking of which, you should know there's a prophecy about you. Well, us. It says that my way to the earth is with the dreamwalk woman who conjures the key. They sent me to find you." He didn't tell her the part about her being in danger, because he didn't want to worry her. Besides, he was there to protect her.

"Oh, *that's* helpful. Sounds like something my grandmother would say." Riya rolled her eyes. "I bet there's a secret oracle's handbook somewhere on how to be obscure."

Idrián laughed. "I think you're right." He looked to his left, then back to her. "I want to teach you about illusions, but this isn't the place for it. Are you up for another trip? We'll go slowly this time."

She held out her hand. "Lead on, MacDuff."

Riya sucked at creating illusions. Idrián's were convincingly solid and detailed, probably because he was a professional artist. He said he could create small ones in the real world, too. Her illusions looked like random blobs of spray paint in the air, probably because her artistic talent peaked with scribbling on the wall with crayons.

On the other hand, she could materialize real objects, like her slingshot, just by thinking about them. It had to be small and something she knew well enough to visualize. She could make her objects vanish, but couldn't do the same with objects that were already in the dreamwalk world, or anything Idrián held, no matter where it came from. After a few tries, she figured out how to materialize objects directly into Idrián's open hand, such as a spoon. She wondered if she was robbing objects from the real world.

"Back in the real world, what are our bodies doing?"

"Sleeping. Dreamwalkers have natural defense mechanisms that wake us up if something is happening to our bodies." He laughed. "When I was twelve, I got a black eye because my cousin woke up suddenly after I put ice down his shirt while he was in dreamwalk."

"What happens if we get hurt here?"

"If you leave dreamwalk before you're healed, you'll have a killer hangover. I'll teach you dreamwalk healing magic." He smiled. "You'll like it. We dance." He raised his hands to the sky and executed an intricate series of steps that she wanted to see again.

A high-pitched sound tickled her ears, like a mosquito at night. She shook her head, but the sound didn't go away. "Do you hear that?"

He closed the distance between them with a powerful leap and put one hand on her shoulder, probably ready to take her out of dreamwalk if needed. Awareness of him flared, but so did the volume of the keening sound that grated on her nerves. He cocked his head and looked left, and she did the same. Some impossible-to-measure distance away, the air distorted like the heat shimmer from desert sands.

"What's that?" she asked. "It looks like someone opened a furnace door."

He shook his head. He didn't seem inclined to go investigate, for which she was profoundly grateful. The keening sound was starting to sputter, like a motor shorting out. Just when she thought to materialize a set of earplugs for herself, the sound dropped in pitch as it faded to nothing. The distorted air smoothed out to clear, lavender sky.

"Maybe we should call it a night," she suggested. She looked up at the now bright yellow sky. "Day. Whatever. If you have to fight, I'd just get in your way."

He gently turned her to face him. "You will never be in my way."

It was the nicest thing anyone had ever said to her. She put her hand on the tattooed side of his face and stroked his cheek with her thumb. The tattoos brightened where she touched him. "Thank you." She loved the feel of his skin. "I'll try not to make you regret saying that."

"I won't. We have a connection. I feel you, even when we aren't touching." He put his other hand on her waist and smiled. "But it's better when we *are* touching."

She stepped in and dropped her cheek to his chest, and wrapped her arms around his waist. "Much better." The scent of him made her lightheaded. She slithered one of her hands lower and under his loincloth to rest on the bare skin of his butt. "Much, *much* better."

"You're incorrigible," he breathed. "I like that about you."

She started to laugh, but the ground shook under her feet, and Idrián tensed. She backed away to give him room to move. The ground shook again, harder, and she heard a sound like something hitting the earth. Idrián pointed toward the direction of the heat wave. "There," he said.

Something was bouncing toward them. It took a couple more thuds for her to realize it was the demon named Moth Dust they'd fought the first night they'd met. The demon landed with a final, earth-shaking whump and focused on her. Its head extended forward on a jack-in-the-box neck. She swallowed.

"Debt acknowledged," said the demon in its incongruously high-pitched voice. From under a flap of skin on its mid-section, it pulled out the red bandanna she'd given it to stanch the blood from its nose.

"Er, yes?" She glanced at Idrián for help, but he was focused solely on the demon.

"Payment offered by Moth Dust." One of its arm-like appendages thumped its hollow-sounding torso. "The T'dzgyiue Existence is missing an *onatec*, who has feet in the Human Existence. It wants not to go home, but instead to bring another of its line into your existence. It rides its steed to open the gate through this plane to invite its *enalpi-ramwo*." It extended the triple-jointed appendage that held the bandanna toward her.

"Ok-a-a-a-y," she said. "Not to be insulting or anything, but I have no idea what you're talking about."

Idrián came to her rescue. "Onatecs are soul-eaters, like Moth Dust is a harshua, a fear-eater. One somehow got to our world, and is working with someone there to bring in a buddy, using dreamwalk as the conduit. Soul-eaters are notorious oath breakers and banished from dreamwalk. They prefer corrupted souls, but they aren't picky and have impulse-control problems. Humans and spirits have few defenses against demons that consider them midnight snacks. One is bad; two could eat stadiums' worth of people."

"What's an *enalpi-ramwo*?"

Idrián shrugged, so she looked to Moth Dust. "Like family." He sneered in disgust. "Vermin. No honor.

Always hungry." It waved the red bandanna at Riya again. "Payment offered."

Riya started to reach for the bandanna, then hesitated. "How do we evict the onatec we have, and prevent it from bringing its whatever?"

"No knowledge. Not my Existence." From which she took to mean that fear-eaters and soul-eaters came from different demon dimensions.

She turned to Idrián. "Warrior." Name magic was powerful in some traditions, so she avoided using his name in front of the demon. "Are we safe if I end this debt?"

He nodded. "Safe enough."

Riya turned back to Moth Dust. "Payment accepted by me, uhm, Dances With Eagles. We are done." She gingerly took the bandanna from Moth Dust's weirdly jointed fingers.

It hissed and bared its lips to reveal crooked, fence-picket teeth, then without warning, bounded up and away, shaking the ground with each bounce as it departed.

The bandanna smelled so bad it made her eyes water. "Someone should explain hygiene to Moth Dust." She held it as far away from her as she could. "Do I need to keep this?"

Idrián winced and waved his hand in front of his nose. "No." She blinked it away, then hastily materialized a wet-wipe towel and scrubbed her fingers.

"So what do we do about the soul-eater?" She blinked the towel away and morphed her clothes into jeans and a T-shirt. "I say 'we' because I'll lay odds this is what the prophecy is about. I'm not really keen on Denver becoming an all-you-can-eat buffet."

He nodded and frowned. "I need to talk to Black Fox." She longed to kiss away his worries, but knew it would only postpone them.

She stepped close to him. "Thank you for showing me all this." She waved to encompass the dreamwalk world. Even without touching, she felt the radiance of him, like the welcome warmth of a fireplace in winter. "Let's go home."

He looked startled, then smiled. "I like the sound of that." He put his hands on her shoulders, and they floated through the sliding-glass door.

7

I DRIÁN ROSE INTO his sprawled body and opened his
eyes, just in time to see Riya awaken with a shiver.
The studio was dark and chilly, and he wished he'd
remembered to warn her about the transition. The feel of
her hand in his made him want to pull her into his arms
to share warmth, but he was embarrassed by how he'd
taken advantage of her in the dreamwalk.

She fished one-handed under the couch for a blanket
and drew it up over herself.

"How are you feeling?" he asked.

"Okay, I think." She glanced at the railroad-style wall
clock, then did a double-take. It was almost midnight.
"We were lying here unmoving for four hours? No
wonder I'm freezing."

He wished he'd thought to warn her about that, too.
"Dreamwalk time is different for each of us. How long
did it seem to you?"

She shook her head. "I lost track. Maybe a couple of
hours? I'll pay better attention next time."

He breathed a sigh of relief as the tension in his shoulders relaxed. At her questioning look, he decided it was better to be candid. "I wasn't sure you'd *want* to go back."

She gave him a big grin and squeezed his fingers. "You're kidding, right? I'd go back just for the wardrobe choices alone." She squeezed again, then let go.

He covered his sharp sense of loss by sliding his legs off the couch and pivoting to sit up. "Bathroom?" He didn't need to go urgently, but it was better to plan ahead. The narrow, antique wrought-iron spiral staircase that rose to her living quarters looked challenging for a man with unreliable legs.

Fortunately, she pointed to a hallway along the far wall. "First door on the left."

When he returned, she was standing, wearing the blanket like a cape. "Do you have a place to stay tonight?"

Yet another thing he hadn't thought of. He was usually better at planning ahead, but the whole trip was rushed and improvised. He shrugged. "I'll find a motel."

She made a face, but said nothing.

"What?" he asked.

"It's just that…" She hesitated and frowned. "I've never had an ounce of my grandmother's oracle talent, so maybe it's because 'soul-eater demon' sounds scary, but the idea of me being alone, of you being alone in a strange town, has me spooked." She pulled the blanket tighter around herself. "Could you be comfortable sleeping on my couch?" She pointed her chin toward it. "It folds out to a bed."

The request surprised him, but it was a good idea.

"Tell her you prefer sleeping in *her* bed," said Black

Fox, whispering theatrically. Idrián jumped, then turned and glared at his grandfather's ghost.

Riya laughed. "Either something just bit you, or Black Fox is back."

Idrián nodded and smiled ruefully. "He has opinions."

She laughed and nodded. "I'll just bet. That's part of why I live in Denver and my parents live on the other side of the world in Perth." She pulled the sagging blanket up again. "So, will you stay?"

"Yes. The couch will be fine." He gave Black Fox a warning look, not fooled by the assumed innocence. Black Fox looked disgruntled as he faded.

Riya's smile was full of relief. "I'll get more blankets." She handed him the one around her shoulders and made running up the spiral staircase look easy. He might have envied her ability, but he was too busy appreciating the perfect shape of her swaying ass as she vanished into the doorway.

"If you'll open the front door," he called up to her, "I'll get my bag from the truck." He didn't want to disturb her wards.

She appeared at the top of the stairs with a bundle of pillows and blankets. "Give me a minute, and I'll key it to you." She threw the bundle over the stair rail onto the well-worn but smooth wood floor below, disappeared for a moment, then came back with sheets, which she carried quickly down the stairs.

She dropped the sheets on the couch, then crossed toward the door and beckoned him closer. "Give me your hand."

He put his hand in hers and instantly felt the connection. She'd said she felt it in their dreamwalk, but he didn't know if that carried over to the real world like it did for him. He'd already rushed things in the dreamwalk; he was determined to take it slower here.

She put her free hand on the door handle, muttered words he didn't catch, then said, "Say a pass phrase."

He thought a moment. "Eaglefoot."

She smiled as she muttered something else. He felt the surge of magic through her and the heavy metal door. She let go of his hand and stepped back. "Try it. Put your hand on the lever and say the magic word."

He did as she asked, and the mechanism audibly unlocked. "How do I lock it again?"

"Tap anywhere on the door twice, then say your word."

He tried it, just to get the hang of it. "Slick spell. Yours?"

"No, I suck at creating durable spells. I traded for it." She smirked. "A dragon shifter was too embarrassed to admit he forgot the combination to his treasure vault, so I opened it for him."

He hadn't realized how versatile her talent could be. "Can you open any door?"

She shrugged. "Most of them. Doesn't stop alarms, though." She laughed. "When I was about four, my cloud-spirit older cousin, who was supposed to be babysitting me, took me to a casino in Monte Carlo and got me to open the bank room, but she didn't disable the alarm. She turned misty and escaped, leaving me, still dressed in my nightie, sitting in front of the open door, crying. My parents were not amused."

He wanted to hear her laugh again, but it was late, so he went outside to his truck for his overnight bag.

By the time he got back, she'd opened the futon, covered it with a fitted sheet, and spread out the top sheet and blankets.

"The big blue jug in the refrigerator has cold water." She'd said her real kitchen was upstairs, but kept a dorm-size refrigerator, microwave, and coffeemaker downstairs. "I have to work tomorrow morning, and I should probably go to the theater early for rehearsal, to make up for ditching last night, but we could have lunch." She shrugged and looked away. "Or not. You've probably got things to do besides visiting the VA clinic."

He gave into the need he'd been denying for the past ten minutes and put his hand on her shoulder. The familiar connection filled the hollow place in his chest. "Lunch would be good."

She slid into his arms with a sigh and rested her head on his shoulder, just like she'd done in dreamwalk. "I'm glad you found me."

He tightened his arms around her. "I'm glad I looked." He rested his cheek on her head, breathing in the scent of her, more subtle and more complex than it was in dreamwalk. "It's been a very long day for both of us."

He reluctantly loosened his hold, and she stepped back and looked up at him with a teasing smile. "God, but you're a handsome man. If we both weren't so tired, and this weren't such a weird way to meet, I'd be putting on some music so we could dance."

"I can't dance." He flinched at the memory of his ex-girlfriend taunting him for it, and dancing with other men because he couldn't. He wasn't handsome; he was damaged. What the hell was he doing?

"Hey." Riya fixed his attention by touching warm

fingers to the scarred side of his face. "I know you can. I've seen you dance in dreamwalk, remember? We'll find what works for you here. Help you find the peace and joy that dance can bring." She smirked. "We can even make you a loincloth if you'd like."

He chuckled in spite of himself. "Gym shorts are a lot more comfortable."

"But not as inspiring." Her eyes twinkled. "Goodnight, my dreamwalk warrior." She kissed him on the mouth before he could react, then twirled away gracefully toward the spiral staircase. "Let me know if you need anything."

He watched her go up the stairs with the feeling that he'd never get tired of seeing her.

The moment she vanished, Black Fox appeared directly in front of him. "What are you waiting for, an engraved invitation? Go after her! She wants you up there in her bed."

Idrián shook his head. "It's too soon." He deliberately walked through Black Fox's ghost toward the refrigerator. It wasn't polite, but Idrián wasn't in the mood for his grandfather's meddling.

"Too soon?" Black Fox sputtered. "It's too late! Women respect a man who takes charge."

Idrián took the jug out of the refrigerator and filled the empty glass Riya had left for him.

Black Fox flapped his hand in front of Idrián's face. "Hey! Rocks for brains! While you're wasting time, your seed is dying. You should be making babies with her while you still can. While *she* still can." Black Fox had become obsessed by the fact that male sperm died every day, a fact he'd learned from educational TV. It didn't matter that new sperm were created every day, too.

Idrián rolled his eyes and carried the glass back to the chair that Riya had pulled close to the bed to serve as a nightstand. "My seed is just fine, thank you." He pulled a telescoping stand out of his bag and set it up on the floor. "Riya will tell me when she's ready."

"Hah!" Black Fox scoffed. "Women don't know their own minds. She just needs an excuse to hump you dry."

Idrián froze in the middle of unbuckling his brace and glared at his grandfather. "If you're trying to make me mad, stop it. If you really meant that, go away and don't come back until you can be respectful to my dreamwalk partner."

"So you do want her." Black Fox looked smug.

Idrián ground his teeth. "You could have just asked." He finished removing the brace and laid it on the floor. The VA clinic had adjusted it so it didn't rub him raw, but now it creaked.

Black Fox vanished for several seconds, then came back. "She's almost naked now, and her breasts are very ripe. Go surprise her."

Overwhelming anger made Idrián surge to his feet. He called up the power of the deep earth and channeled energy to the fingertips of his left hand, turning them molten red. "I will court this woman my way or not at all." His left eye twitched.

Black Fox's chin thrust forward pugnaciously. "You're wasting your real-world magic on a spirit you can't touch. You're afraid she'll reject you."

"That's my problem, not yours." Idrián made a fist, not caring that the skin of his palm stung with heat. "If I ever find you spying on her again like some perverted skin-walker, or saying anything to hurt her, I will find your grave in dreamwalk and burn it to ash." He opened his fist and splayed his white-hot fingers.

"Lazy, cowardly, selfish boy," Black Fox snarled. "The death of the To'Piro tribe will be on your head!" Black Fox conjured a storm ball in his hand and threw it at Idrián's chest, then vanished.

Cold water hit the heat of his hand and instantly became steam, drenching him with the mist. Idrián was too mad to be impressed that Black Fox had figured out how to manifest more than his ghost image in the real world.

8

I DRIÁN SAT IN the theater audience again, this time visible to anyone who looked. He was pleasantly full after a late buffet lunch of East Indian food, which he'd never tried but found he liked. If he was honest, Riya's company would have made even military rations palatable.

She still didn't seem to see his injuries, but as usual, others did. He was used to the sidelong looks, avoidance, and inappropriate comments. She wasn't.

"He's so brave, going out in public like that," a woman in the buffet line had said to Riya, apparently unaware they were together.

"Yes, he's very brave," replied Riya, her tone overly innocent. "Women throw themselves at him all the time. He has to beat them off with a stick." She leaned in and lowered her voice confidentially. "Why do you think he carries a cane?"

The startled woman turned red and found an excuse

to leave the line. Riya shook her head and muttered about some people's children.

He'd enjoyed the rest of the meal, bantering back and forth with Riya about what they were eating and trading stories of their encounters with strange foods in other countries. He got the impression her parents were wealthy, which had him wondering why she was living like a starving artist in a quasi-industrial neighborhood. He couldn't think of a way to ask that didn't sound judgmental or mercenary.

At the theater, he asked her for a grand tour, mostly as a way to spend more time in her company. He found himself constantly making excuses to touch her, and she responded by moving closer to him, brushing dust off his shoulder, or slipping her hand into the crook of his elbow. When their skin touched, the connection came alive, but he was even feeling hints of it from a few feet away.

She introduced him to the theater's technical director, then showed him the dressing rooms, and pointed out the technical booth, above and behind the audience, where the lights and sound operators worked their mundane magic.

Once they got to the backstage area, they found set pieces stacked haphazardly in one of the wings and a rolling rack overstuffed with hanging costumes. She swore.

"St. Peters should be here, organizing this. Whitney said he canceled last night's tech rehearsal after I left." She pushed some small but heavy boxes of printed programs out of a marked traffic lane. "If I do it, I won't get paid for it and that sleazy bastard will get all the credit. If I don't, tonight's rehearsal will be a disaster." She sighed and crossed her arms grumpily. "I'm screwed either way."

He pulled her into his arms and kissed her forehead. "I don't know enough to fight this battle for you, but I'll have your back."

After a moment, she relaxed and wrapped her arms around him. "You say the nicest things to me." His body responded to hers immediately with a flood of heat that sent his blood straight to his groin. He'd been semi-aroused since the first time he'd seen her in person. And when he was miles away, like his morning's trip to the VA medical clinic, she was always on his mind, like an unforgettable song.

Her phone played the famous ominous opening notes to *Toccata and Fugue in D Minor*, and he felt her tension return. She sighed as she pulled away a little so she could dig in her bag. "It's Denise, the executive director. May as well get this over with."

He started to step back, but her grip on him tightened. He was happy to stay where he was, connected with her. He listened unashamedly as she politely but firmly strong-armed the director into meeting her at the theater. She ended the call, then kissed him on the cheek. "Thank you for being here."

"My pleasure." He brushed back a wisp of her hair that had escaped her bun. The turquoise ends reminded him of her sleek feathers in dreamwalk that tickled his skin teasingly. "I know you have things to do. Should I get out of your way?"

She gave him a cheeky grin. "You'll never be in my way." The same words he'd said to her the night before in dreamwalk. Her expression softened into seriousness.

"You're my rock. I didn't think I wanted one until I met you." She kissed his lips lightly, as if they'd been together forever. "I hope that doesn't scare you off."

"Nope," he said. He smiled crookedly. "Black Fox says I have rocks for brains."

She laughed. "Is he here? I don't see him."

Idrián shook his head and couldn't keep the frown off his face. It had taken him a good hour to cool off after their argument, and he was still simmering. Black Fox wasn't always an easy man... spirit to live with.

She started to speak, then seemed to think better of it. Instead, she gave him a long, tight hug. He wanted to sweep her off her feet and carry her to the couch he'd seen in the pink-and-yellow room she'd inexplicably called the "green room," but he couldn't figure out how to carry her and his cane. He took solace and delight in the feel of her against him.

She kissed his chin. "If you want to sit, the best places are the dressing rooms or the house, where the audience sits."

"The house would be safer, I think." He didn't want to distract the other dancers. Besides, he wanted to ask the factory worker ghosts for a favor, and he needed quiet to do it.

Safely ensconced in the back row in the same seat he'd been in yesterday, Idrián squeezed Riya's hand. She sat next to him, waiting for the executive director to arrive. She stroked the back of his hand with her thumb. "The last row of a movie theater was where I had my first kiss."

"Mine was the playground of Magic's elementary school. She was so startled she shifted into her weasel form and bit me." Because events before his last tour in Afghanistan seemed like someone else's life, he didn't often talk about his past, but she made it seem more real.

Riya laughed, and Idrián decided he was addicted to the sound of it. His former girlfriend's laugh was always mean, usually at someone else's expense. Riya's laugh sounded like spring and sunlight, and he wanted to hear it often. He fought his impulse to pull her into his lap and give her a kiss that would obliterate the memories of anyone else's but his. *Take it slow*, he ordered himself.

She gave him a sidelong glance. "Can I ask you something?"

"Anything." He wanted no secrets from her, except maybe how much she already meant to him. He'd even tell her the details of the incident that took his lower leg, and the long road back, if she wanted to know.

She squeezed his hand. "Do we have a connection here, the same as in dreamwalk? Or is it wishful thinking on my part?" Her expression was vulnerable, the first time he'd seen it in her.

He lifted her hand and pressed a kiss on the back of it. "It's very real." He loved the soft smile on her face.

A voice that was little more than a breeze with vowels and consonants whispered in his ear. *"An angry woman is in the lobby."*

Idrián nodded his grateful respect. The ghosts of the factory workers didn't like trouble in their midst.

"I think Denise is here." He kissed the back of Riya's hand again, then released it.

"Thank you." Her smile was fleeting as she stood and

squared her shoulders, then exited the row and stood at the top of the aisle, facing the lobby.

Denise turned out to be a short, plump woman in tall shoes and a severe black suit. She zeroed in on Riya and immediately went on the attack.

"The board is very disappointed in your behavior, Riya, and so am I." Indignation and condescension colored her tone. "Canceling last night's rehearsal wasn't within your authority, and you were insubordinate with Jonathan." The corporate-style phrasing was undoubtedly designed to imply Riya's job was on the line.

Riya looked singularly unintimidated. "Only insubordinate? I was going for hard-ass bitch. He told Spencer Emerson that he choreographed *Red Dust Warrior*." She crossed her arms. "If he told you I canceled rehearsal, he's lying."

"He said Mr. Emerson didn't believe *Red Dust Warrior* was yours. Jonathan said he gave you credit." Denise shook her head. "You didn't hear all of the conversation."

Riya frowned, and Idrián wished he knew whether or not to come to her defense. The choice was taken out of his hands when Denise finally noticed his presence and rounded on him.

"You can't be in here, sir." Her frosty tone brooked no argument. "You'll have to leave."

"He's my guest," countered Riya. "He's my combat consultant and Native American culture expert."

Denise frowned and started to speak, but he beat her to it. "I overheard all of Mr. St. Peters' conversation with Mr. Emerson last night. St. Peters said the choreography was all his, and that Riya only did the rehearsing." He cast a quick illusion to keep the left side of his face in shadow, so she'd focus on his words, not his appearance.

She looked taken aback for a moment, but regrouped quickly and turned back to Riya.

"There, er, must have been a misunderstanding." She raised her chin condescendingly. "You haven't acted professionally, but I'm willing to give you another chance to show the board you deserve to be considered for the artistic director position."

Something in Denise's words caused Riya to narrow her eyes. "Really." She cocked her head a little sideways. "Second thoughts about giving my job to St. Peters?"

Denise's jaw tightened, like she wanted to bite something. "He missed two interviews this morning and a sponsor luncheon. He's not in his hotel room, and he's not answering calls or texts. And he hasn't been in an accident that we know of."

"Hmm." Riya met Denise's gaze head on. "What do you want me to do?"

"Handle all the production stuff"—she waved fingers vaguely toward the stage—"so we don't have to refund tickets."

"How much does it pay?" Riya's tone was deceptively mild.

Denise looked relieved. "I'm sure we can arrange something after—"

Riya interrupted. "Now, or never. I'm not lifting a finger until I get a new, fully approved contractor agreement that spells everything out, and none of the 'other duties as assigned' clauses like you put in my old agreement. You can pay me the same as St. Peters."

Denise pursed her lips sourly. "Prorated."

Riya's smile turned predatory. "Sure, if you pay me for the *two months* I've already been doing the job, and you cut a check tonight." She stared steadily at the other woman.

Denise glanced at the empty stage, then heaved an aggrieved sigh. "Deal." She pulled out her phone. "I'll get the agreement and a check to you in the next couple of hours." She started stabbing the screen of her phone as she turned and exited into the lobby.

Riya sat on the arm of the nearest aisle seat. Idrián stood and exited the row as fast as he could. "You're shaking."

"Adrenalin. I'll be okay in a minute. I don't like fights." She sighed. "No way they'll give me the job after this. Not sure I'd take it, either. I guess this is Fate's way of telling me it's time to look for new opportunities."

He nodded as solemnly as he could. "Been there, done that, got the wooden leg."

She laughed, as he'd hoped. "Come on, Mr. Funny Guy." She stood and kissed him on his jaw. "We've got another hour before the dancers get here. Help me figure out how to organize the set pieces, and I'll show you the best places in the theater for making out." She waggled her eyebrows suggestively.

It was his turn to laugh. "I like your priorities."

9

"TOP OF THE show in ten." Riya raised her voice so the dancers, who all stood on the stage, could hear. She turned and gave a thumbs-up to the crew in the booth and the stage manager in the wings, who'd luckily been as easy to work with as her company of dancers.

When everybody had arrived, she'd promised them the blessings of the Hindu dance goddess if they got through the technical rehearsal and a run of the concert in full costume. She'd been diplomatic about St. Peters' absence, but she knew everyone was as relieved as she was that he wasn't there. With Idrián's permission, she'd introduced him as her friend and "intern," which made everyone laugh, then bluntly explained his injuries so he wouldn't have to repeat the story a dozen times.

Luckily for her, Idrián turned out to have decent carpentry skills, which meant he could help assemble the standing set pieces, and she put his artistic talent to good use in fixing a backdrop so the large, rearing stallion painted on it had the usual four legs instead of three. She didn't try to hide her attraction to him or their nascent relationship, knowing her friends would figure it out anyway. The only fibs she told were pretending they met on the internet instead of a magical plane between worlds, and that he'd come to Denver to see her dance, not because of a prophecy by a five-hundred-year-old ghost.

"I'm going up front to check that the box office is locked," she told him, putting her hand on his arm because she wanted to feel the connection. She thought she was starting to be able to tell where he was even when she couldn't see him, but she sternly warned herself that might be wishful thinking.

"Okay." He leaned closer and whispered conspiratorially. "Does it have any spots for making out?"

She laughed. "Let's go see."

The lobby was deserted and dark, but streetlights shone through the wide bank of front windows, making it feel like a fishbowl. After confirming the box office door was locked, she checked the lobby doors, too, then crossed to Idrián to stand just a few inches in front of him. "Hi there, handsome."

He put his hand on her shoulder. "Whatever they're paying, you deserve double."

She smiled. "Thank you. You're seeing us at our worst because we're having to cram two nights' work into one. Tomorrow will be better." She dropped her forehead to his shoulder. His presence played merry hell with her concentration, but she wouldn't trade it for anything.

"Thank you for not treating me like an invalid."

She looked up at him, surprised. "It never even occurred to me."

"I know." He smiled and kissed her lightly.

She slid her hands onto his hips and hooked her thumbs into the belt loops of his jeans. She wanted him with an intensity that made her heart race and her belly tighten. "After we're done here tonight—"

A loud knocking on the glass interrupted them. A man and a woman in suit coats stood at the door, staring at them.

Riya moved closer to the door to yell through the glass. "Sorry. The theater is closed."

One of the men lifted a lanyard and pressed the identification and a badge to the glass. It said he was Detective Wayne from the Denver Police Department.

"Riya Sanobal?" he shouted. "Denise Moreland said to ask for you."

Riya turned her head toward Idrián. "What do the factory worker ghosts think?" she asked quietly. She knew he'd asked them to be sentinels, since he couldn't set wards on a large public building.

"They're human. No magic," he murmured.

Riya turned the deadbolt knob to unlock the door and pulled it open to admit the two detectives.

"Are you Riya Sanobal?" asked Wayne. He was tall, balding, and wore round-frame glasses. His companion was younger, dark blond, and considerably leaner than the pot-bellied Wayne.

"Yes. How can I help you?"

"I'm Detective Wayne, and this is Detective Sundstrom. We'd like to talk to everyone who was here last night. Ms. Moreland said you'd all be here."

"We are... well, except for Jonathan St. Peters."

Wayne exchanged a meaningful look with Sundstrom. "We know."

Riya didn't need her grandmother's prognostication talent to know it was bad news.

According to the police, Jonathan St. Peters had been found murdered in an abandoned warehouse in an older industrial district near the railroad tracks. From what the police *weren't* saying, Riya gathered the death had been unpleasant. She'd never known anyone who'd been murdered. Even though she heartily disliked St. Peters, he didn't deserve that.

Wayne asked her about the fight she'd had with St. Peters the day before, and what she'd done the rest of the evening. She told them frankly that St. Peters had tried to take credit for her work, and she'd told him to come clean or else, then spent the rest of the evening with her friend and houseguest, Idrián. They took a photo of his identification, but didn't seem interested in him, perhaps because he was just visiting and perhaps because all they saw were his injuries.

According to the dancers, St. Peters had announced his new position and said Riya had taken the news badly and stormed out. He'd received a text message around six-thirty and told the dancers and crew he had to run an errand, and to start the tech rehearsal without him. They'd done what they could, but when he hadn't come back by eight-thirty, they'd locked up and left.

Riya was sorry the man was dead, but he was still a lazy jerk.

Sundstrom showed everyone selected digital photos of the warehouse where St. Peters' body had been found, and asked if they recognized the symbols painted on the floor. The police apparently thought they were made up, but Riya recognized them at once as magical in nature, and she knew from a quick glance at Idrián that he did, too.

Under pretense of needing better light to see the photos, she took Sundstrom's tablet to the stage manager's station, where she used a small spell to send all the tablet's photos to an encrypted shared internet storage location that her family used for private affairs. Her father's cloud-spirit family had invented cloud storage long before humans got around to it. She wanted her very magical parents to look at the symbols, but first, she needed to warn them that some of the photos might not be for the weak of stomach.

By the time the police left with complete contact information for everyone, it was almost nine o'clock.

"We have three choices," she told the group. "Do the full run-through like we planned and stop for problems, do an entrances-and-exits run-through, or give up tonight as a lost cause and make do with the full dress-and-makeup rehearsal tomorrow."

Whitney raised her hand. "I vote we do a full run-through tonight, but marking where we can." The other dancers quickly agreed, and the crew said they'd stay, mostly because she promised overtime pay. With a new, fat check in her bank account from Denise, she could afford to pay them herself if she had to.

Riya nodded. "Okay, five minutes to places. Warm up

when you can. Write down non-critical problems on the stage manager's clipboard."

Fortunately, she had time to take Idrián to one of the dark corners she'd promised him. In between a few hot kisses, because she couldn't resist, she told him about the photos she'd copied.

"Could you email them to my cousin Román?" he asked. "He's a genius with languages and spells."

"Sure, text me his address."

"What's 'marking'?" His warm, capable hands caressed her back and gently kneaded the knots he found there.

"I'll give you an hour to stop that." She leaned into him gratefully and let his fingers work their physical magic. "Marking is doing the movements, but not with full energy or intensity. It's safer when dancers are tired or distracted. We all have regular jobs so we can pay the rent, so it's been a long day for us." She moaned softly while he worked the sore muscles below her shoulder blades, where she often carried tension.

She kissed along the left side of his jaw and came to his deformed ear. Carefully, in case the area was painful, she touched it lightly with her tongue. He shivered and tightened his grip on her.

"Okay?" she asked.

"Better than okay," he breathed, his voice deep and rumbling.

"We'll save it for later," she promised. He'd already found a couple of sensitive spots on her, so she was glad to have sensual ammunition of her own.

She reluctantly sent him out into the audience to watch so she could focus on her work.

Riya waited until she saw Whitney and Mack, the last to leave, get in their separate cars, then locked the front lobby door and went back into the theater to meet Idrián at the backstage doors. She found him muttering, and assumed he was talking to the factory's ghosts. She was hungry and tired.

He turned to touch warm fingers to the side of her face. "Let's get food that's bad for us and go home, oh highly underpaid woman."

She chuckled. "Can't argue with that." She opened the door and gestured for him to go first. She closed the door firmly shut after them, checked it to be sure, then used her magic to make doubly sure that all doors were locked, especially the alley door the dancers sometimes used to step outside for a moment and forgot to close.

By the time they got to her place and parked their vehicles, she'd already wolfed down all of her ultra-sized order of fries and half her burger. She laughed when she saw Idrián had done almost the same.

She pointed to the several dabs of paint on his forearm. "Do you want a bath tonight?" Heat rushed to her face when she imagined him gloriously naked, and helping him wash every part of him. "I, uh, my shower isn't big enough for a chair."

"Yes, a bath would be good." He tilted his head toward her loft apartment. "The circular stairs will be a challenge for my legs. Could you carry my bag up?"

She blushed again. "Sorry, yes, of course. I didn't even think." She was a babbling loon.

"Just this once," he responded with a twinkle in his

eye, "I'll forgive you for not anticipating the need for accessible stair design for a total stranger who dropped in on you out of the blue."

"You're too kind." She chuckled. "Go on up. Light switches are on your left, and the bathroom is the first door on the right after the kitchen. Ignore any clothes you see on the floor. They have parties when I'm not home."

As she collected his bag and hers, she deliberately didn't watch him navigate the staircase because she didn't want him thinking she thought he was incompetent. When she'd remodeled the warehouse to suit her, designing for the disabled hadn't even crossed her mind. She needed to remedy that, and soon.

Assuming, of course, that Idrián would ever be back again. They'd only just met, not counting dreamwalk time, and lots of things could go wrong. The sizzling desire that had kept her engines revved for the last twenty-four hours was a shaky foundation for a relationship. He lived five hundred miles away. She had to get through all the performances and look for a new place to dance. He had ranch responsibilities that she, a city girl, couldn't even imagine.

Her parents would want to meet him, and that was the tip of the iceberg as far as dealing with her challenging family. The spirits of his ancestors might reject her for her non-human heritage, despite her dreamwalk abilities, and she knew their approval was important to him.

And despite her alibi, she might be a person of interest in a murder case.

The sound of running water drew her out of her spiral of doubts. She knew where she wanted to be right then—

upstairs, where the man she'd been dreaming about was getting naked.

She knocked on the closed bathroom door. "I'll leave your bag outside the door."

"Could you bring it in?"

She left her bag in the hall, then opened the door to find him seated on the edge of her large, antique claw-footed bathtub, wearing only boxer shorts. His brace leaned up against the rim. The extent of the burn scars didn't surprise her, because she'd seen them as the living tattoo in dreamwalk, but seeing his human legs did. She blushed when he caught her staring. "Sorry, I guess I was expecting feathers and talons."

He snorted. "Is that how you see my legs in dreamwalk?"

She blinked. "Don't you?"

"No, they're just my legs. My prosthesis translates to a sort of realistic mannequin's leg with a hinged ankle." He splashed his hand in the bath water, then adjusted the hot-water faucet. The play of his lean abdominal muscles made her breath catch.

"What about your burn scars? I see them as tattoos that are constantly moving, telling a story." She blushed again. "They lit up where I touched you, like one of those old mood rings."

"I see them as they are here. Could I have the metal stand out of my bag?" He nodded toward the bag she was clutching to her chest.

"Sorry." She put the bag at his feet, then found the stand and handed it to him. It put her close enough to catch his scent, and despite her exhaustion, her hormones woke up. She stepped back quickly, before she did something stupid. A flash of hurt crossed his face before he smoothed it away. Did he think she was repulsed by him?

"Idrián, I love it when we touch." She took a deep breath and let it out slowly, deciding to take a chance on honesty. It was easier to say what was on her mind in the ephemeral world that was dreamwalk, but it felt important to say it in the physical world. "You're sexier here than in dreamwalk, and that's saying something." She swallowed, her throat suddenly dry. "It scares me, wanting you this much, because I want more than wicked-hot sex with you. I want to build a relationship that lasts, and I don't know if that's what you want. So when I back off, it's not because I don't want you, it's to stop from throwing myself at you and going up in flames."

Wordlessly, he set the stand on the floor, then stood and held his hand out to her. She took it and let him reel her in as he stood and wrapped his arms around her. Two thin layers of cloth did nothing to hide his body's reaction to her, or hers to him. She pressed her cheek to his shoulder and enjoyed the sensations.

"I want all that." He rubbed a gentle circle on her back. He probably meant it to be soothing, but her hormones begged to differ.

She gathered her courage and looked up at him. "Will you share my bed?"

His eyes widened. Then he kissed her, hard, and she met him with neediness of her own. He tasted of heady desire. Her breasts felt swollen, aching for his touch, his lips, his tongue. She grabbed the hand that was caressing her ass and put it on her breast to give him the idea.

A distant clatter reminded her where they were. With

as much willpower as she could muster, she pulled her mouth away from his. "Bathtub. Water."

The dazed look faded from his eyes as he processed her words. "Right."

He started to twist around, but she beat him to the faucets to shut off the flow. His chest was heaving for air as much as hers was.

"As much as I'd like to continue this," she said, putting a palm on the pectoral muscle of his chest, "we shouldn't waste the hot water. My water heater is old and slow."

He slid his hand under hers to capture her fingers, and a corner of his mouth twitched. "Is this a subtle way of telling me I stink?"

She laughed. "No. All my friends will tell you I slept through subtlety class." She took a step and picked his leg brace off the floor from where it had fallen, and leaned it against the rim of the tub again. Reluctant to lose the last bit of contact with him, she stretched out her leg to hook her foot in his open bag and drag it close to the tub. "The sooner you're done in here, the sooner we can pick up where we left off."

She backed up a step and released his hand. Their connection energy dropped but didn't fade to nothing as it had before.

"Out," he mock growled, then gave her an evil grin. "Unless you'd like to watch?" He slowly slid his thumbs under the waistband of his boxers and started to tug them downward.

"More than anything. I love burlesque." She signed and pointed to the tub. "Sadly, hot water waits for no man." She turned to leave, then turned back. "The bedroom is at the end of the hall."

She scooped up her bag and marched to the bedroom. If she'd stayed a moment longer, she'd have been helping him out of his boxer shorts with her teeth, and she didn't want their first time to be on the hard, cold bathroom tile.

She switched on the light and was relieved to discover she hadn't left a horrendous mess. She dropped her bag to the floor inside her walk-in closet, then pulled off her clothes and dropped them into her hamper. Growing up around shifters, she was comfortable with nudity, but he might not be, so she put on a nightshirt. She wanted to seduce him, not shock him.

As she turned back the covers, she remembered she hadn't told her parents about the police photos. She pulled her notebook computer out of her bag and sat with it on the edge of her bed. She composed the message to her mother asking for translation and information on the magical symbols, with a warning the some of the photos might be grisly, then used her magic to send the message to their family cloud net. She got Idrián's cousin's email address from her phone and sent same message and the photos to him. She plugged both devices into their chargers and put them on her tall, narrow dresser.

She sat on the edge of the bed to wait. A wave of exhaustion ran through her, making her realize she was nearly at the end of her reserves. She closed her eyes. Four more days, and the concert's run would be over, and she could think about what to do next. Whatever it was, she wanted it to involve the clever and sexy man in her bathtub…

The next thing she knew, Idrián was gently shaking her shoulder. "Riya, lift your legs."

She realized he was trying to get the blankets out from under her. She rolled over onto her back and looked up at him blearily. The only light was coming from her bedside table. "Sorry, I must have fallen asleep."

"Shhh," he said softly. He was half-kneeling beside her, wearing nothing but thin cotton shorts. His damp hair was slicked back into a ponytail. He slid the covers down, then guided her feet under the sheet.

"Please stay?" she asked hopefully.

"All right." His voice soothed her.

She dozed until he slid his hips down and lay flat on his back, his arms up behind his head. She rolled on her side, then oozed herself into the solid warmth of his body, twined her leg with his, and rested her head on his chest.

Nothing had ever felt as perfect as that moment. She tried to hang onto the bliss even as she sank into oblivion.

10

For the second day in a row, Idrián had slept the whole night through without once being awakened by phantom pain in his nonexistent foot, or bad dreams, or even an unfamiliar bed. It took him a moment to realize he was alone in that unfamiliar bed, and that it was close to nine o'clock in the morning.

His bath the previous night had taken longer than he'd realized, because the tub had high sides and the hot water felt so good. He'd taken the opportunity to clean both his stump and his socket liner with antiseptic, and dry his hair enough so it wouldn't drip. By the time he'd put his leg back on, put all his stuff back in his bag so it wouldn't be in her way, and taken it into the bedroom, he'd discovered Riya had turned into sleeping beauty, slumped to the side with her bare legs still on the floor. He would have made the trip back downstairs if she hadn't asked him to stay. The contact and her warm breath on his chest lulled him into a deep sleep.

He discovered a note on the bedside table that listed

her insanely busy schedule, told him to feel free to make breakfast for himself, and apologized for not having a TV. She hoped he'd come to the theater after three, if he had time.

Time was the one thing he had plenty of. Ordinarily, he had chores at the ranch to keep him busy, but all he had in Riya's reclaimed warehouse were his thoughts. He hadn't even brought his ereader.

He called Rollie and Hanif to check on things at the ranch and remind them about keeping the goats penned, and told them he'd likely be gone a few more days. Smartass Rollie figured out Idrián's emergency involved a woman and pried mercilessly, but Idrián refused to give him any details.

He checked his email and responded to a few, including one from his cousin that complained about the poor quality of the police photographs. Román was working on a translation, but he was unhappy that the symbols were blocked in several shots. For all that Román's suave good looks had girls practically claim-jumping him in high school, and had unexpected success as a composer, he was a geek at heart. He was probably so focused on the symbols he didn't even notice that it was blood or a piece of human flesh obscuring the symbols.

There was no polite way to describe what happened to St. Peters' body; it had been shredded. Not even a feral bear or tiger shifter could do that kind of damage. Idrián hoped St. Peters had been dead before the dismemberment.

He still had several hours to fill. He wanted to save dreamwalking for when he could do it again with Riya. His business with the VA was done. He debated finding a nearby gym, but he wasn't in the mood to be stared at. Still, he needed to exercise almost every day or he'd become the actual invalid that most people saw when they looked at him. Accordingly, he improvised some weights and used Riya's springy wooden studio floor.

As he worked through a borderline-painful routine designed to keep his right leg mobile, he distracted himself with the memory of the *Red Dust Warrior* piece she'd choreographed. He didn't know the first thing about dance theatre, but her piece was stunning, noticeably different from the others. St. Peters at least had the good taste to steal from the best.

The lead dancer, Mack, who played the warrior, had partnered with her in a later piece she danced in, and needles of jealousy pierced Idrián's heart. Mack was tall, supremely graceful, handsome, and outgoing. All Idrián could claim was being tall. He soothed himself with the fact that Riya had slept last night in his arms, not Mack's.

If Riya was interested in Mack, there was nothing Idrián could do about it, except maybe call his earth magic and heat the asphalt enough to flatten the man's tires.

Idrián groaned. He was acting like a lovesick werewolf.

He refilled the blue water jug for the downstairs refrigerator, then carefully walked up the circular stairs to her kitchen. He changed into his jeans and a T-shirt, wishing he'd packed more clothes, or at least underwear. It occurred to him he could go for a drive and find a coin-op laundry, so he shoved everything in his bag and slung it over his shoulder. It would be better than counting the minutes until he could see Riya again.

Idrián parked his truck in the back of the theater as Riya had instructed, then knocked on the backstage door. She opened the door immediately. Her hot pink, camouflage-pattern T-shirt said "Whiskey Tango Foxtrot," and her faded black jeans were so splattered with paint, they looked like the Milky Way galaxy on a clear desert night.

"Hi there, handsome man with food. I think I felt it when you arrived." She touched her chest, then his. "Is that normal?"

"I don't know." He smiled and kissed her, because he could. "I've never had a dreamwalk partner. I feel it, too."

She took the takeout salad and iced tea she'd asked him to bring, then led him back to the room with an ugly but serviceable couch and invited him to sit. He'd already eaten, so he waited while she ate the chicken strips off the top of her salad, then wolfed the rest of it down, too. It should have been boring, but he enjoyed being in her company.

A factory spirit wearing overalls and boots drifted in and hovered near the door. Idrián nodded to the ghost in silent greeting.

To his surprise, after Riya finished eating, she kneeled on the couch beside him and crawled into his lap. "Hi." Their renewed connection hummed in his chest and settled his restlessness. "I didn't want to leave this morning."

"I'm sorry I didn't wake up." He'd even slept through the sounds of her morning shower and a coffeemaker loud enough to rouse the neighborhood.

"I'm not. Well, I am, because I'd have liked to fool

around, but you needed the rest, and it was my turn to open the coffee shop." She nuzzled into his neck, her breath warm on his skin.

"Do you need to work?" he asked.

She laughed. "Very diplomatically put." She sat up a little and looked him in the eye. "Yes, I need to work. Money complicates things worse than sex ever does." She touched fingers to the scarred side of his face. "I love my parents, but if I took money from them, it'd be a license for them to start meddling in my life. If I lived off my trust fund, I'd never know if someone hired me to dance because they liked my talent or my bank balance." She snorted. "Hell, my last loser of a boyfriend saw me as a meal ticket because I had a steady job at the coffee house. I'd have never gotten rid of him if he'd known my family has money."

"I know what you mean. I don't have money, but my last girlfriend wanted the ranch, or more specifically, the land, and had to pretend she wanted me to get it." He smiled wryly. The difference between her and Riya was night and day.

"Pretend?" Riya's eyes narrowed. "She'd better be long gone, or I'll close every damn one of her doors."

"Don't worry." He kissed her cheek to soothe her heart-warming fierceness. "She burned enough people that the Magic town council specifically excluded her from the invitation. They don't do that very often."

"The invitation?"

"When the town was built in the seventeen hundreds, the founders created an invitation that went out to all magic users, the non-humans, the persecuted, the feared, to come settle in a town where their differences would be more than welcome." He brushed a strand of hair away from her face. "You've probably felt it and didn't know it. You're here in Denver, when you could have picked anywhere else in the world. Sooner or later, you'd have found a reason to be in southern New Mexico, and you'd have stumbled across the town."

"Hmm." She tilted her head. "When I selected the music for *Red Dust Warrior* and sent the permission request to the composer at a New Mexico address, I came really close to taking a long weekend vacation to see the landscape that inspired the piece."

He smiled crookedly. "The Fates have been busy. My cousin Román is the composer." He didn't like being manipulated, but he couldn't complain if it brought him Riya. "He's too pretty. I'm glad I met you first." He kissed her. She responded instantly, and desire lanced straight to his groin. He deepened the kiss and slid one hand under her T-shirt to feel the warmth of her soft skin. She gasped and arched into him.

"Higher," she breathed. "I've been wanting you all day."

He slid his hand up to cup her generous breast. Her nipple tightened diamond hard when he brushed a thumb across it through her sports bra. He adjusted his hips to give his growing erection room, and groaned when her clever fingers rubbed him through his jeans. His hips involuntarily thrust into her touch. He was perilously close to losing it right there.

Sounds of men's voices broke through to the few thinking parts of his brain. Someone was calling Riya's name.

She must have heard them, too. "Dammit, it's Mack and Kenji. They're early." She kissed him, wet and sensuously. "We will continue this, I promise." She kissed his nose. "Just not for a live audience."

She clambered off his lap to stand and straighten out her T-shirt. He pulled out his own to hide the bulge in his jeans. "I'll be out in a few minutes."

She gave his left thigh a quick caress, then left the room. The ghostly factory worker in overalls gave Idrián a commiserating look.

In the next hour, he helped Riya take care of most of the items on her checklist, from putting cases of bottled water in each of the dressing rooms, to gluing a large fake jewel on a headdress, to rummaging in the theater's supplies closet for an extension cord.

She put glow tape on the floor to mark where set pieces would go, helped Kenji figure out how to wear his demon costume, answered the sound operator's questions, and set up a table for props. In between, she found odd moments to make a physical connection with him, laughing when he brazenly stole a kiss.

As he was taking extra folding chairs to the women's dressing room, he ran into Mack, who was wearing a sleeveless tank top and low-slung tight pants covered with sleek feathers.

Mack grabbed the last two chairs from the cart and followed him in. "It's probably none of my business, but I'm going to say it anyway. I've never seen Riya looking so happy, and I think it's because of you. She's a class act, so she probably won't tell you, but her last boyfriend was a cheating slime, and I'll regret introducing them for the rest of my life. So, thank you for treating her right."

Idrián nodded, not missing the implied warning that if he didn't treat her right, Mack would make him sorry.

"She's an extraordinary woman." He took the chairs from Mack. He unfolded the first chair, then looked at the handsome, healthy dancer. "To be honest, I thought you might be more her type."

Mack shook his head. "Nope. We'd drive each other crazy in under a week." He unfolded the chair in his hands. "I'd rather have her as a friend."

Idrián unfolded the last chair. "I'm glad she has good friends."

"We wouldn't have a company without her." Mack shook his head. "Denise owes her serious groveling for the way they screwed her over."

Riya's voice came over the speakers in the dressing room. *"Mack, we need you on stage."*

Mack headed for the door, stripping off his tank top as he did. "Coming, Mother!" he shouted.

Idrián chuckled, as much from Mack's irrepressible good humor as from relief that Mack wasn't competition for the woman that was increasingly in Idrián's every waking thought.

As soon as the other dancers began to arrive, Idrián found a seat in the first row in the house. Between his morning exercise and helping Riya, he was getting a full day's workout, almost as good as riding Patli to the mountain and back. At well after seven, his stomach was reminding him that it expected to be fed. He wanted a chance to take his leg off, too, because sweat was collecting in the socket liner.

Riya came toward him to sit on the edge of the stage. "Hey there, handsome."

"Hey, yourself." He leaned forward to get up, but stopped when she jumped down and sat by him. He offered his hand, and she took it. Their connection flared, as it did each time they touched skin to skin. "So what's the schedule?"

"I need to get into costume and makeup. Curtain is at eight, intermission at about nine-fifteen. If things go right, we'll all be out of here by ten."

His stomach growled, and she chuckled. "Interns are allowed dinner breaks."

"What about you?"

"I can't eat and dance. I'll get something on the way home." She leaned closer and whispered in his ear. "Just so you know, I plan to have my wicked way with you tonight."

He squeezed her hand. "I'm up for that." He waggled his eyebrows.

She laughed. "I'm counting on it."

She stood, but didn't let go of his hand. "Come on, let's walk to your truck, and I'll tell you the restaurant options around here."

11

A FTER HE KISSED Riya goodbye half a dozen times, because once wasn't nearly enough, Idrián decided on a restaurant with a drive-through, even though it was several miles away. He was tired of fast food, but he didn't want to be stared at or treated like he was breakable. He appreciated how easily the dancers had gotten used to his looks, because of Riya, but they were exceptional people.

It took longer than he planned because he overshot a turn and had to take a longer way around, so it was after eight by the time he got to the food delivery window. His phone had rung earlier, but he'd let it go to voicemail, rather than chance an accident.

He stopped in the restaurant's parking lot to listen to a message from Riya. Denise had arrived moments after he'd left to announce that a big sponsor—the Spencer Emerson Trust—had donated an eye-popping figure for a special group of rich friends to be given exclusive viewing of the rehearsal. The catch was that no one else would be allowed in the theater or backstage, including friends and family of the dancers. Riya gave him the option of coming back to the theater at nine-thirty, when the rehearsal finished, or meeting her at her apartment later. Riya commented that rich people were crazy, and that she missed him already.

Idrián didn't like it. He hadn't forgotten that the main reason for the mad dash up to Denver was because of Tompiro Spider Woman's warning that Riya was in danger. He felt guilty that he hadn't told her that part of the prophecy, and now she didn't know to be watchful. He sent her a text message saying he'd come to the theater at nine-thirty, and not to leave without him. Her reply said the alley door would open for him, which probably meant he could sneak in earlier. He didn't want to get Riya in trouble, but he wasn't going to leave her unprotected at the theater, either.

He choked down his sandwich and chips quickly, then drove back to the theater and parked in the back lot. After a long moment of thought, he fished in the inside pocket of the emergency backpack he kept behind the seat and pulled out a small medicine bag his grandfather had made for him.

He breathed life energy into the bag, then put its lanyard around his neck. "Grandfather, I ask forgiveness for my angry words, as I forgive you for yours." He added a touch of earth magic to his voice, to send it through both dreamwalk and the spirit world. "Black Fox To'Piro, I would ask your help in protecting the dreamwalk woman."

Because he was paying attention, he knew Black Fox was there before he spoke. *"It's about time you came to your senses, Eaglefoot."*

Idrián ignored the verbal jab. "Do I need to catch you up, or have you been watching the whole time?"

Black Fox's spirit materialized into view and shrugged, unabashed. "I heard her message."

Idrián nodded. He got out of the truck, grabbed his cane, and walked toward the alley. He hadn't needed to use it as much lately, but he wanted to look harmless if Denise or the sponsor caught him.

The door opened with his touch just as Riya had promised. He put a small rock in the frame to keep it from closing all the way again. He stood in the darkened hallway, listening intently, but all he heard was noise from the air vent. He should have been hearing music, or voices, or something. He whispered a greeting to the factory ghosts, but got no response.

Black Fox appeared in front of him. "Go to the stage. No need to be quiet."

Idrián walked as fast as he could, his leg brace creaking. Black Fox preceded him. "Riya?"

"Not here."

Idrián almost tripped, but continued forward. He broke into an uneven half run when he saw the stage manager slumped in her chair. Beyond her, the bright stage lights revealed an eerie tableau.

All of them, including Denise and the crew, were sprawled on the stage, as if they'd all decided to take a nap. A quick check of the first two dancers proved they were asleep, not dead, but unresponsive. More bizarrely, three faint factory-worker ghosts were similarly slumbering. Just as Black Fox had said, only Riya was missing.

Panic rose, but Idrián firmly pushed it aside. He bent down to Mack's sleeping form and called the man's name.

A whiff of the grave threatened to empty his stomach and he reared back. "Corpse magic."

Black Fox stood in front of him as he stood. "We can't stay, or it will trap us, too." He pointed in the direction of the alley door. "Riya's portal spell is fading."

Idrián wished he could stay and help the dancers, but Riya came first. He could feel the weight of the sleep spell eroding his energy reserves, making his limbs feel heavier. He determinedly started back toward the alley door, only deviating from his course when he glimpsed Riya's orange and purple bag and snagged it. Something personal of hers might make her easier to track.

The darkened hallway toward the exit seemed to stretch out for a mile. He doggedly put one foot in front of the other, keeping his eye on the sliver of fading daylight that outlined the open door. He used the discipline forged by hundreds of hours of physical therapy to ignore everything but reaching his objective. He staggered into the door's push bar and stumbled out into the alley. He turned to see Black Fox's spirit form flicker like a strobe as he struggled against the perimeter of the spell. Idrián called magic from the earth and thrust his fingers back through the open doorway and into his grandfather's image. He gritted his teeth against bitter cold and held fast until Black Fox made it over the threshold, then blinked out.

Idrián used more earth magic to warm his hand as he walked as fast as he could toward his truck. He opened the door and threw Riya's bag and his cane in, then climbed into the driver's seat and shut the door. Black Fox materialized in the cab, perched on Riya's bag.

He needed a destination. *Think*, he ordered himself,

closing his eyes. Riya had said she felt his location, so he had to believe that would work for him, if he could get close enough. He snapped his eyes open and looked at his grandfather. "How do I find Riya in dreamwalk? I told her to go there if she was ever in trouble."

"From the heart," said Black Fox. "Every dreamwalker sees it differently, but it comes from the heart."

Idrián wasn't practiced at plunging into dreamwalk while behind the wheel of his truck, but desperation made it one of the fastest entries he'd ever done. The familiar red earth and opalescent skies soothed him, but his worry skyrocketed. He dropped to one knee and bent down to put his hands on the dry dirt to ground himself and his runaway emotions. He focused on memories of Riya, remembering how it felt when they touched in dreamwalk, how it energized every cell in his dreamwalk body and filled his hollow chest with warmth. The ground warmed beneath his left hand. A skipping line of energy appeared, like the pattern a sidewinder snake made in the desert sand. He followed with top dreamwalk speed as it made a path through the landscape. It was headed toward the rocks where they'd first met and defeated the fear-eater demon.

To his overwhelming relief, she was sitting in the center of the half ring made by the rocks, her arms around her legs, her chin resting on her bent knee. He slowed to normal speed and let the world stabilize.

"Riya," he said softly, walking toward her.

She looked up and smiled tiredly. "Hey there, handsome. I don't think I can stay here much longer."

He dropped to his knees and gathered her into his arms. Immediately, he felt the drain, dragging at him through their connection. He pulled energy from the earth and funneled it to her.

She snuggled into him. "That feels good."

"I can't do it for long. Your body wants you back. What happened after I left?"

"Spencer Emerson came in, all alone, and asked everyone to come to the stage. When we did, he spoke a word of power to freeze us all, then cast a spell to make us all sleep. The bastard picked me up like a sack of rice and carried me out over his shoulder. I wasn't fully under, but his touch made me so sick I could barely breathe or keep my shields up. As soon as he got me into the back seat of his big SUV, I remembered what you said, that you'd find me in dreamwalk, so I opened the door and ran." She drew in a ragged breath. "I ended up here."

He kissed her head and tightened his arms around her. "Did Emerson say anything?"

She snorted. "You mean something helpful, like where he was taking me, or why?" She rested her head against his shoulder. "No. But remember what Moth Dust said, about the soul-eater demon 'riding its steed' to open the gate? I think Emerson is the demon's meat puppet." She sounded exhausted. "I really hate being part of a prophecy."

He smiled. "They do tend to be hard on the people involved." The drain grew stronger, and she started to fade. He struggled to hang on to her a moment longer. "I'm coming for you, Riya."

"I'll try to open a d..." Her body dissolved into nothingness, leaving his arms empty and his heart aching. He should have protected her better.

He drew as much more earth energy as he could stand and shot up into the sky...

...and slammed back into his body, gasping for air, pins and needles dancing on his skin. He took several more deep breaths to settle the extra earth energy into his bones and joints, making them ache.

The clock on his dash said he'd been gone less than twenty minutes, the fastest dreamwalk he'd ever done, but after seeing Riya's haggard look, even that felt too long. The truck cab was empty. Black Fox must be doing something he thought was important.

Hoping he was doing the right thing, Idrián pulled Riya's sweater out of her bag, then got out of the truck and crossed to the tiny bit of turf that surrounded a small tree. He sank to one knee to get more contact with the soil, then focused on the same connection to Riya he'd made in dreamwalk and tried to feel it through the earth. The deep vibration of the city thrummed in his veins. He concentrated on her exotic scent, the taste of her on his lips, the moisture of her breath on his skin as she'd slept in his arms. He sent a tiny thread of magic into the ground and willed it to find Riya. It snaked out slowly, headed southwest, then faded. He poured more magic into it, but it didn't go much farther.

Frustrated, he balled up Riya's sweater and held it to his chest, then concentrated once more on the remembered essence of her. Nothing.

Every second of delay pounded on his conscience. She'd been taken because of his arrogance. He should have told her about the danger. He should have protected her. He should have told her he was falling for her.

The realization stunned him. It was too fast. It wasn't safe. He needed more time. And none of those arguments changed the fact that he'd already given her a piece of his heart.

His grandfather's instructions came back to him. He took a deep breath, sent his magic out again, and poured his feelings for her into it.

The thread shot out like a laser, southwest, and terminated nine miles southwest of where he knelt. Memorizing the feel of it through the earth, he hurried back to his truck and used his phone's map to plot the quickest route to get there. He took a moment to cast a quick spell to set off the fire alarms in the theater building, so someone would find and help the stricken dancers. It was all he could do for them for now.

He roared out of the parking lot, engaging the truck's magical systems to hide it from traffic cameras and make other drivers choose to get out of his way without knowing why they did it.

Given the location, Idrián suspected Emerson, or the demon that rode him, liked decrepit warehouses and railroad tracks. Idrián drove past the building that his magic said was his target and parked on the far side of a rusted van that made his truck look pristine by comparison. A fast, northbound train thundered by on the tracks to the west of the row of warehouses.

Black Fox appeared just as Idrián opened the glove box to get a multi-tool with a few extra features.

"I asked the ancestors for advice. They don't agree on anything except that you must keep your connection to the earth and bring your woman to the ranch." Black Fox frowned. "I can't tell you what you'll find in the warehouse. It's warded against spirits."

"How many doors?"

Black Fox vanished, but returned quickly. "Six, counting the three freight bays. The door at the south end has footprints leading to it."

Idrián nodded his thanks. Impulsively, he grabbed Riya's sweater and tied its arms around his waist. If... no, *when* he found Riya, she might appreciate the warmth. He braided his hair quickly, whispering a small spell into it, leaving it one word short so he could trigger it if he needed it.

Idrián got out of the truck with his cane. He breathed fog on the side mirror and drew quick symbols. The truck faded from view.

"How will you get in?" asked Black Fox.

"Riya said she'd try to open a door for me. If not, I'll think of something." He started a fast walk toward the south door. "Coming?"

Black Fox glided beside Idrián. "Don't get us killed."

"You're already dead," Idrián pointed out.

"Smartass," growled Black Fox. "There are worse things than death."

12

Riya was wet and cold, owing to the mildewed blanket on the chilly concrete floor Emerson had left her on. She was trussed painfully with duct tape, her arms behind her, and tied to her ankles with more duct tape. The center of the dark warehouse was lit by standing banks of work lights, each unit plugged into a car battery, with a spell on each to convert the power. The warehouse smelled like a dust, mold, and ancient grain, but that was overwhelmed by the stench of death magic and demons. Plural.

Now that she was looking, she could see the demon wearing Spencer Emerson's skin, especially since it wasn't trying to hide its inhuman occupancy like it had in Denise's office.

It stank of human sweat because it had been hard at work, pouring magic into the symbols it was painting on the floor in six concentric circles around Riya. The expensive tailored suit coat and pants it was wearing were ruined with paint smears. Apparently, soul-eater demons were rock stars that trashed their metaphysical hotel rooms.

The other demon was about the size of a German shepherd, but pallid pink, with clawed appendages, multiple eyes, and ripping teeth as big as her forearm that made no sense to her human sensibilities. It sat just beyond the edge of the blanket and glared evilly at her. Or maybe it just had a resting evil face.

"You're quiet," said Emerson, as he dipped his paintbrush into the tube of red acrylic paint. Ever since he'd pulled her back to the real world using a spell that would have awakened Rip van Winkle, he'd been chatting with her like they were at a party.

She rolled her eyes. If he wanted conversation, he shouldn't have put duct tape over her mouth. Maybe it was just as well, though, because she doubted she could have suppressed her undiplomatic comments. Her shoulders ached, and her fingers felt icy cold from lack of circulation. She wished she knew what time it was.

Another train, this one northbound, rattled the warehouse walls and vibrated the concrete floor.

The smaller demon made a slurping sound. "Humans, soft." It gnashed its teeth, which sounded like breaking glass. "Hungry, me."

Riya wished she had something to block the fetid odor of its breath. It knew better than to come closer. When she'd first come to, the demon, whose demonic name sounded like Yellow Snow, tried to sneak in and take a bite out of the meaty part of her calf when Emerson wasn't looking. She'd kicked at it with her bound feet, but it was the static electricity shock that sent him skidding ten feet along the floor, and smeared some of Emerson's symbols in the process.

Emerson had kicked it until it was screaming and bloody, or at least she assumed the black, oozy fluid was blood, and threatened it with true death if it touched her or the symbols again. Interestingly, Emerson hadn't commented on the magic spell she'd forgotten was still active, the one that had kept Jonathan St. Peters from bothering her. Or maybe her little spell was beneath the demon's notice.

"St. Peters was whimpering by now." Emerson stood and stepped back to survey his handiwork. "It would have been much easier if he could have finished the dance. His was quite the tasty little corrupt soul. Yours isn't."

From Emerson's running conversation, she'd gathered he'd lured St. Peters to the other warehouse the night before, nibbled on the rotted parts of his soul, taught him the movements, then convinced him to dance while Emerson cast the gate spell. Unfortunately, St. Peters had neither the talent nor remaining life energy to keep the gate open, and only Yellow Snow had made it through. St. Peters was already comatose when Yellow Snow had chewed through St. Peters' flesh before Emerson could stop it. Apparently, manifesting bodies in the human world sent juvenile soul-eater demons into an uncontrollable frenzy until they got used to the sensory overload.

Emerson daintily stepped through the rows of symbols and crouched down in front of her. Without warning, he ripped the duct tape off her face. She gasped involuntarily with the pain, and her eyes watered.

"Are you a better dancer than St. Peters?"

She didn't say a word. Her only hope was delaying things as long as possible, to give Idrián time to find her.

The demon that was occupying Emerson made the man's mouth smile. "I'll make it worth your while. I'll give you anything you want. I'll make you a ruler." He made a complicated gesture with his fingers, and Riya felt a wave of seductive persuasion wash over her like a warm sea as she glimpsed a brief illusion of her wearing a fairy-tale crown, looking down from a balcony over an adoring crowd.

Riya couldn't help but snort. She'd always looked ridiculous in princess dresses. "I'm guessing St. Peters fell for that bullshit?"

Emerson blinked, then shook like he was having an epileptic seizure, dropping to his knees. It took her a moment to realize the demon was laughing. "Yes, he did. Hook, line, and sinker."

The demon Yellow Snow drooled. "Eat now!"

Without looking, Emerson grabbed Yellow Snow's barbed head and flung it up and over the circle of symbols into the darkness. It landed with a crunch and a howl.

Emerson cocked his head to one side. "You see the real me, don't you?"

Riya knew the demon meant itself, not the human fleshy shell it operated. She wondered who the real man had been. He was probably long gone. "Yes, I see you. Sort of." Best not let it wonder what else she could do. "I don't know why, though. I've never been psychic or anything, except for seeing the odd ghost."

Emerson crossed his arms. "Dance for me, and I'll let you live."

"Liar." Riya sneered just as disdainfully as she had when calling St. Peters on his theft.

Emerson lifted his right hand. "I will sign an oath in blood." His voice sounded deep and sincere, but it didn't match the eyes. Whatever demon was wearing Emerson's skin wasn't doing as well at keeping up the human façade.

She remembered Idrián describing soul-eater demons as oath breakers and shook her head. "Oaths aren't worth the paper they're written on. I learned that lesson cosigning a loan for my cousin."

Emerson slapped her, hard, slamming her head into the hard concrete, then grabbed her chin and forced her to look at him. "I can make you immortal and bend you like a pretzel. You'll have pain forever. You'll never walk again, much less dance."

Her eyes filled with involuntary tears. Her nose dripped. Being crippled was her secret fear, the threat her insane, rabidly anti-human uncle used to torment her with when her mother wasn't around. It had driven her to figure out how help the wounded and the maimed learn to move again, because she was afraid she'd be the one with the mangled legs or the twisted spine. She shivered.

But if she gave into her fear, hundreds would die. Courageous, strong, warm-hearted Idrián, who'd miracu-lously come back from a devastating loss, would die. After all he'd been through, he deserved life. She couldn't let him down.

Riya swallowed hard and looked up into the eyes of hell. "Do it."

Emerson stared at her a long moment, then curled his lip and pushed her chin away. He wiped his fingers on his stained pants.

Relief flooded her. For whatever reason, Emerson's demon needed her cooperation. All she could think of to do was play for time. "Why do you need me to dance?"

Emerson sat back on his heels. Slowly, the demon's countenance overlaid Emerson's. It was rounded, almost doll-like, with eyes, nose, and mouth in a human configuration. "I want to go home."

The tiniest bit of doubt began to nibble at her resolve. What if the soul-eater demon really did want to go back to its own dimension?

"What's your name?" she asked.

Underneath her, through the concrete floor under the thin blanket, she felt a tiny, magical vibration. The south warehouse door opened, the one she'd spent all her waking minutes and spare small magic keying to open for Idrián without disturbing the demon's wards. She coughed to hide any hope that might be flaring in her eyes.

"Derorril. Onatec ..." The demon trailed off and sniffed the air once, then again. "Yellow Snow, bring me the spirit that is stupid enough to invade my territory. Do not eat it yet." The little demon scrabbled fast, and flew upward on wet-looking wings into the darkness.

The demon retreated into the Emerson shell. "Is someone looking for you?"

Riya gave him a sour look. "Like you'd believe me, no matter what I said."

Emerson frowned. "You're annoying. More than most." A slower southbound train rattled the walls of the warehouse. Underneath its vibration, she felt the south door close again. She needed to keep Emerson busy.

She made a rude noise. "It was your dumb question. If

I said yes, the police are coming, you'd think I was lying, and if I said no, you'd still think I was lying." She sighed in exaggerated exasperation. "You obviously haven't been here that long, or you'd have figured out by now how to ask a decent question. Now, if you'd asked—"

A bright flash and an earsplitting howling rose from the east side of the warehouse. Yellow Snow flew into view and crash-landed at the southern edge of the circle of symbols. Its right wing was ruined by a huge, jagged burn hole, like it had been struck by lightning. Black blood pooled on the floor, and it crooned its agony.

"Heal yourself," ordered Emerson. Yellow Snow crooned louder and rocked itself.

"Must I do everything around here?" Emerson's body shook as Derorril emerged as a greasy black cloud, then formed into a taller, long-tailed, deep pink insect-like creature with an incongruously cherubic but insectoid, face. It shook itself and stood up straight and stretched, as if it had been stuck in a cheap seat for a transcontinental flight. The body was semi-transparent, sort of like a hologram instead of the real thing. The demon peered into the darkness toward the east, then unfurled huge wings and launched into the air.

Yellow Snow quieted, but still rocked itself.

Riya expected Emerson's body to fall, now that it was unoccupied, but instead, it continued to shake. It also heaved like a cat with a fur ball. She barely squirmed herself and her blanket away before he leaned forward and spit up a dark red slimy mass on the concrete, just inside the center ring of symbols. She carefully avoided looking at it, but she couldn't avoid the smell of sickness and death. Her stomach heaved in revulsion.

He sat back on his heels and wiped his mouth with the sleeve of his coat, smearing yellow paint across his cheek as he did so. He finally noticed her.

"Who are you?" He looked blearily around. "Where are we?"

"In a warehouse near railroad tracks, maybe near South Santa Fe."

His eyes widened. "We're in New Mexico?"

"No, Santa Fe Drive, in Denver. Are you Spencer Emerson?"

"Call me Spence." The reply sounded automatic. "Where's that pink bastard?" He struggled to lift a knee to get his foot under him, but he seemed not to have the strength.

"Chasing a ghost, I think." She tried to smile winsomely, knowing she probably looked like hell. "Could you cut the tape on my wrists? There's a box cutter in your left pocket."

He absently put his hand in the pocket and pulled out the box cutter, but it slid from his fingers when his whole body twisted in sudden, harsh spasm. It looked painful, but seemed to bring more lucidity as he peered at the floor. "Those are dance magic symbols from my grimoire. I have to get out of here."

He tried to stand, but his legs buckled under him, and his knee landed on the box cutter. He swore as he picked it up and tossed it on to the blanket. "What's today's date?"

"May fifth. Could I have that box cutter?" She pointed with her chin.

Spence swore viciously. "The greedy bastard is burning through my store of life force like there's no tomorrow." He doggedly got to his hands and knees. "Don't believe anything he says. Serves me right for not paying attention to which body I was raising. I just wanted a few stock tips. How was I supposed to know the moron hedge-fund manager had been dabbling in black magic and got himself possessed?"

He pivoted southward on his knees and froze. His gaze locked onto the injured Yellow Snow, who was slowly creeping toward them. Spence snarled a curse that caused the demon to curl into a small ball and whimper.

The psychic stench of death magic—necromancy—made Riya shiver. Now it made sense that Spence survived possession by a soul-eater demon. Necromancers were immune to soul stealing.

Crackling and hissing erupted from the darkness in the southeast end of the building. It galvanized Spence, who turned in the opposite direction and started crawling slowly across the symbols, smearing globs of paint as he went.

Riya desperately rolled over on her stomach and tried to aim her hands where the box cutter had landed. She forced her circulation-deprived fingers to feel around behind her, and tried not to imagine accidentally groping the disgusting red slime expelled from Spence's stomach. She felt cool metal and fought against the blanket to wrap her fingers around the handle.

An inhuman scream reverberated in the warehouse. She rolled over again so she could see what was going on and scrambled to hide her prize under a blanket fold. A tingle of awareness trickled through her, meaning Idrián was near. She'd give anything to be in his arms right then.

Derorril limped into view, a fading burn mark on its

leg, dragging something after it. The demon slid its burden onto the symbols, then leapt to stand in front of crawling Spence. "Going somewhere?"

Riya's attention was on the misty figure the demon had dragged in. Her heart sank when it solidified enough for her to recognize the face of Black Fox. The middle of Black Fox's chest was impaled with a giant stinger, with a slimy ectoplasmic thread that led to Derorril's tail. She felt guilty that she was relieved it wasn't Idrián, who she knew was to the west of her, beyond the pool of light.

Black Fox was clearly in agony as he tried to pull the stinger from his chest, but it wouldn't budge. The effort appeared to exhaust him. He cast Riya an apologetic look.

She looked at Derorril just in time to see it shoving itself back into Spencer Emerson's shuddering, trembling body. It rose to its feet and bounced a couple of times, as if to seat itself in Emerson's form.

Derorril looked calculatingly at the spirit of Black Fox, then toward the darkness. "I feel your connection, mage. Come out where we can see you, or I'll have my *enalpi* eat the remains of your ancestor."

Yellow Snow scrambled to its feet. "Hungry!"

While Emerson's attention was on the warehouse, Riya slid her uncooperative fingers under the blanket and pushed the slider on the box cutter to expose the blade. She clumsily turned it and started sawing at the tape, hoping she had the sharp edge pointed the right direction.

"I'm losing my patience, mage." Emerson crossed his arms and tapped his foot.

Yellow Snow drooled. The hole in its wing looked significantly smaller and less singed than before. It started slyly edging toward Black Fox's prone form. Black Fox floated closer to Emerson.

She sawed as hard as she could and felt the tape start to part. It spurred her to work faster, even though her wrist tendons were straining, and the returning circulation was torturous. She gritted her teeth to keep herself from crying out in pain.

From out of the darkness, Idrián finally spoke. "I'm coming."

The tape on her wrists gave way. She winced as she slowly moved her arms forward to relieve the strain on her shoulders.

Idrián limped slowly into view, his brace creaking, leaning heavily on his cane. He stopped once he was fully in view, with the scarred side of his face lit by the harsh work light. His pant leg was partially hitched up as if by accident, exposing his prosthesis. She guessed he was giving the demon reasons to underestimate him.

"You're tall enough, but you're damaged beyond repair." Emerson looked him up and down. "Why don't you stupid humans cull your injured? It's not like there aren't billions of you."

Idrián shrugged. "Tall enough for what?" He glanced briefly at Black Fox, who was still transfixed by the monstrous ghost stinger.

"To be my next ride, of course." Emerson raised his hand and looked at the back of it. "I'm tired of cramming myself into this one. I can't eat it, and it keeps fighting me. Besides, it's running dry. I'm not going to wait until it's out of life force and get stuck buried in a box under-ground again. Another stupid human practice." He tilted his head back toward Riya. "She's young and healthy, but her body is even smaller than this one."

Even the implied threat to her had Idrián's expression hardening, and she felt their connection energize, the way it had in dreamwalk when he'd called up earth magic to share with her. He was about to throw himself into the fray to protect her, and she couldn't let him sacrifice himself.

She sat up and cleared her throat loudly. "What do you need another ride for? I thought you wanted to go home."

Emerson turned to her. "I do." His eyes narrowed when he saw her pulling the duct tape off her wrists. "Will you dance? Open the gate for me and Yellow Snow?" Beyond him, she saw Idrián subtly shake his head.

Riya made her decision and hoped it was the right one. "Yes, if you let the mage and his grandfather's ghost go."

"What are they to you?" Emerson peered at her suspiciously.

"Not much, really. I just met them yesterday." Riya shrugged. "They meant well." She'd make it up to Idrián later for making him sound unimportant and ineffectual. If there *was* a later.

Emerson nodded solemnly and held up his hand like a scout. "Very well, I promise."

She laughed without mirth. "You'll have to do a lot better than that."

It took thirty minutes of arguing to convince Deror-ril/Emerson to agree to let Idrián leave the warehouse.

She used every ounce of acting ability she had to convince the demon she was smart enough to negotiate a good deal, and naïve enough to believe that when she opened the gate, he and Yellow Snow would go home quietly.

Fortunately, the demon's considerable power made it arrogant, and it clearly didn't understand humans, even though it was occupying one. She let it assume that Spence-the-necromancer had cut her loose, and that Idrián's magic had breached the warehouse boundary. The more the demon underestimated her, the way it had Idrián, the better.

"The mage must swear a blood oath not to interfere," said Emerson, "or the grandfather ghost will be Yellow Snow's next dinner."

Riya wasn't sure the smaller demon could actually eat spirits, but she couldn't take the chance with Black Fox's safety. She heaved a theatrical sigh. "If the *vision* of him leaving makes you happy, I'm sure he can do it." Dammit, why couldn't she have telepathic powers, or know a spell to tell Idrián what she was planning? He wouldn't *like* her plan, but maybe he'd stop looking so angry and despairing. She couldn't afford to look at him very often, because she knew her feelings for him would show on her face, and that would give Emerson an advantage.

Thankfully, Idrián seemed to have caught on. He pulled a multi-tool from his pocket, opened a thin blade, and pricked his finger. "I swear by the graves of my ancestors not to interfere in your quest to go home. You can watch me drive away in my truck." He turned the bleeding finger to face Emerson, then flicked the blood droplet away. "I want *your* blood oath to free Riya and my grandfather's spirit once the gate is open."

Emerson pulled the box cutter out of his pocket, which he'd retrieved earlier, and sliced the meaty part of his palm. Blood welled, and he flicked it onto the concrete. "I swear by my blood that the woman and your grandfather will be free once the gate is open." The cut was already healing by the time he slipped the box cutter back into his pocket.

Idrián gave his grandfather one last look, then turned and limped slowly away past the haphazard ring of standing work lights and into the darkness.

Riya cleared her throat. "So what's this dance you need me to do?"

Emerson turned to her with a deep frown. "I hope you're a better dancer than St. Peters. He kept trying to take shortcuts."

Riya twitched a sardonic eyebrow. "Story of his life, I'll bet."

Emerson's body shook with Derorril's laughter.

13

T HE HARDEST THING Idrián had ever done was walk away from the two people who meant the world to him. His grandfather's spirit was suffering, and Riya was playing a deadly game. He'd been ready to attack when the demon in Emerson's skin threatened her, but he had to trust that she had a plan. A better plan than his, which mostly consisted of plowing in and smashing things. That worked when driving Army tanks in Afghanistan, but not against powerful demons.

The second he heard Riya's question about the dance and the demon's laughter, he picked up speed and half ran to the south door, muffling his footsteps and creaking brace as he went. He needed time to craft the illusion Riya had asked for, of him driving away in his truck. This wasn't a little illusion like a blood drop on his finger for a meaninglessly vague oath. It was bigger than any he'd ever done in the real world before, so he hoped the dark, moonless night would hide any flaws. It was only possible now because of his growing connection to

Riya, his dreamwalk partner. He wished he'd thought to tell her they were already making each other stronger, able to use more of their dreamwalk skills in the real world.

He opened the warehouse door and fused the hinges with earth heat so the door would stay open. He cloaked himself in darkness beside a pallet of rotting cardboard, then gathered as much earth magic as he dared. He quickly constructed an ethereal armature, blew dust onto it, and shaped it into an image of himself, then sent it limping out the door. The demon's wards flared.

He hastily built his truck illusion in front of the rusty hulk of a van. Just in time, too, because Emerson came to the door to watch illusion Idrián get into the illusion truck and drive away. Idrián made sure the demon got a good look at the illusion's unhappy face.

Emerson glanced up to the moonless night, then tried to shut the door, but Idrián's handiwork held fast. Emerson kicked the door in frustration, then spoke a word of power to strengthen the wards and headed back toward the center of the warehouse.

Even as Idrián watched, Riya's subtle portal magic began undermining the wards, warping them upward by tiny increments. After only a few moments, something mouse-sized could cross the threshold. Not that there were any of those left. He'd found tiny carcasses earlier that he suspected were victims of the smaller winged demon.

Idrián cloaked himself in his best concealment spell and slowly crept along the west wall, past a rusty, boarded-up train-loading door. Any faster, and the movement of magic might be noticeable. Several minutes later, he was close enough to see Riya and the two demons, and the hazy outline of his grandfather's ghost.

"...more complex than the first four. Show me that sequence again," said Riya. Her dusty turquoise hair was half falling out of its bun, her T-shirt was damp with sweat, and she was barefoot. Her shoes and socks were piled to one side.

Emerson gestured, and a conjured sexless figure executed a series of steps and body movements.

Riya danced. The fourth ring of symbols lit up, joining the first three, with a few blanks where symbols were damaged or obscured. Emerson used magic to repair the darkened symbols and they lit up, too. Only one more ring to go.

Emerson nodded, then gestured again. "Next." The sexless figure danced. To Idrián, the sequence looked both long and difficult.

The collected but unfocused power coming from the rings beat against Idrián's senses. It felt almost like dreamwalk...

Idrián could have kicked himself. It *was* dreamwalk. Soul-eater demons couldn't manifest in the human world directly; they needed black magic or the dreamwalk for passage and translation to physical form.

When entirely human and already weakened St. Peters had danced the previous evening, the gate, which Idrián and Riya had seen as heat shimmer in dreamwalk, had only stayed open long enough to allow one small demon through.

When resilient, talented, portal-mage Riya's dance lit the final ring, the twenty-foot-wide gate would slice through dreamwalk like butter.

"Dance," ordered Emerson.

"Show me again." She wiped the sweat off her forehead and used the hem of her filthy T-shirt to dry it.

"You're being slow and stupid on purpose." Emerson pointed at her feet. "Dance!"

Riya's eyebrows rose. "Oh, so it's okay to improvise?" She did a quick series of small movements. Seven of the previously lit symbols went dark.

"Stop!" Emerson stomped across the pattern and stared at the dark symbols. "How did you do that?"

Riya shrugged. "No clue. It's your spell." She pulled the hair band off her head and slicked her hair back. "Unless you bought it off the internet, in which case, I hope you went to a reputable dealer. That dark net stuff is downright dangerous." She replaced her hair band. "So, do you want to show me again, or should I just make more stuff up?"

Emerson glared as he stopped at each symbol to use his magic to light them again. After the fifth symbol, his shoulders drooped, as if running out of energy. He repaired the last two symbols, then gestured, and the sexless figure danced.

Riya made him show her three more times. Emerson kicked the smaller demon off the outer ring of symbols and stood outside the ring, staring avidly at Riya. "Dance!"

"Fulfill your oath. Free the ghost." She pointed to Black Fox, who was barely moving and looked pale and blurry.

Emerson shook his head. "Not until you complete the dance and open the gate."

"Then move him to the center with me, where he'll be

safe." She crossed her arms, making it clear she wouldn't budge.

The unfulfilled magic potential in the room made the hair on the back of Idrián's neck stand on end. He fought the urge to put his hands over his ears, because it wouldn't help.

Emerson stomped his foot in annoyance, but gestured toward Black Fox's form. The ghostly figure floated toward Riya, but stopped when the ectoplasmic thread between Emerson and the stinger impaling Black Fox drew taut. He was still over the first ring of symbols.

"He's safe now," announced Emerson. "Dance!"

Riya started the sequence. This time, with each movement she completed, a symbol in the outer row lit up, and the fifth, then fourth, then third rings grew brighter and shifted from cool white to a deep reddish-pink tinge.

Wind emanated from the floor, blowing up dust and debris. A high-pitched keening bypassed Idrián's ears and drilled straight into his skull, like a slow-motion percussion wave from a roadside bomb. He gritted his teeth and shook off the traumatic memory.

Riya froze in mid movement, her left leg bent high in the air behind her, her torso leaning forward, her arms outstretched, her face to the floor. "Free the ghost."

Emerson stomped in a mad frenzy. "Don't stop now, stupid human. You'll kill us all!"

The power charge in the room pulsed, like a lightning bolt gathering to strike.

Riya held her pose. "Free the ghost." Her fingers shook with tension.

With an inarticulate snarl, Emerson gestured and yanked on the ectoplasmic thread. The stinger wrenched loose from Black Fox's chest and retracted under Emerson's suit coat and vanished. The cloudy wisps that made up Black Fox oozed past the rings into the center.

Riya continued the dance. The symbols lit and the rings brightened. It felt like dreamwalk was bleeding into the real world, calling him, inviting him to join with it. He anchored himself to the real world with more earth magic.

In a fast flurry of movement, Riya completed the sequence, then dropped to one knee. The rings turned deep red as they connected to one another and became solid walls that sank downward. Riya and Black Fox huddled in the dangerous eye of spinning, howling gale-force winds that rattled the entire warehouse, but didn't affect Emerson or the smaller demon.

Emerson exultantly looked down into the gateway in front of him, where roiling red and black clouds were rising.

Because Idrián was watching Riya, he saw that under the cover of slipping on her shoes, she'd started dancing again, with small movements of her head, torso, shoulders, and hands. The color of the walls started shifting to pink and gray, and the winds slowed a little.

Blankets of cotton-candy-pink fog overflowed the edges of the gateway, where they began forming into dozens of small knots of clouds, about the size of geese, that coalesced into stomach-churningly ugly, pale pink demons with multiple mouths and eyes, clawed limbs, and distorted horns. Though they were pink, they looked nothing like Emerson's big demon or Yellow Snow. Their bodies twitched and shivered.

Emerson glanced behind him at the little demons,

then did a double-take. "No, no, no, no, *no!*" He kicked several of them back into the gateway, but the winds blew them back up into the air, where their round bodies tumbled like balls in a lotto machine. He shouted something in a demon tongue, but it didn't seem to stop more pale-pink fog from pouring out. Growling, he spoke a harsh word of power so weighty that it drove him to one knee. It washed over the warehouse like the wave of an earthquake, and Idrián fought to stay still behind his concealment spell.

The gateway collapsed. The space became the floor of the warehouse once more, and the winds around Riya and Black Fox died down. She was on one knee, tying her shoe, breathing heavily. Black Fox hovered over her shoulder, looking better than before, but not well.

The sudden quiet lasted only one long moment. Three of the newly formed round demons screamed like peacocks. One started bouncing. Another rolled. The third began hitting itself, drawing green blood. More demons started screaming. A fourth demon rolled to the third demon and began slurping up the spilled blood.

Idrián remembered story lessons taught to him by the spirits of his oldest ancestors, about the small, pale demons that had once overrun dreamwalk and devastated the land that later became the American Southwest, destroying multiple settlements. If these were the same, they'd be like a very large pack of locusts, eating everything living in their path.

Emerson got to his feet. "Quiet!" He spoke a word of power that had all the other demons, including Yellow Snow, cringing and whimpering. Emerson staggered toward Riya and Black Fox.

"You will die. Slowly. On a spit." The demon's translucent tail emerged from under the suit coat and curved up and over his shoulder, like an eight-foot-tall scorpion's stinger. "But first, the meddling ghost."

"Stupid demon," sneered Black Fox.

The demon's tail struck with blurred speed, but Black Fox vanished. Riya tried to evade the stinger, but it went right through her... and had no effect.

One of the round demons began repeating the words "on a spit." Several others took up the chorus. "Ghost," chanted others. "Stupid demon."

Black Fox appeared behind the demon and drew lightning from the blackness above. "No brains at all." He directed the spirit lightning directly onto the demon's tail. The demon yowled as its ghostly stinger charred and smoked. Black Fox vanished again as Emerson spun to look for his tormentor.

"Brains," repeated dozens of the round demons, sounding like a cheap zombie film.

Idrián suppressed a jerk when Black Fox appeared next to him behind the concealment spell. "I'm spent, Eaglefoot. I'm going home."

"Wait," breathed Idrián. "Before you go, tell Riya we've got some of our dreamwalk powers here. She doesn't know she can defend herself."

"Your woman is braver—" began Black Fox.

Idrián didn't have time for another lecture on his inadequacies. "Than me. Yes. Please tell her."

Black Fox frowned as he faded away.

Emerson turned back to Riya. "Fine. I'll deal with you." He began a low, chanting spell that congealed the air in Idrián's chest.

Riya mouthed her own spell. Idrián badly wanted to go to her, to face the demon together, but it would be suicide. He tried to send her some of his earth magic through their connection, the way he'd done in dreamwalk, but he couldn't tell if it worked. He couldn't send her much, or Emerson would notice the foreign magic in his temporary demesne.

Black Fox appeared next to Riya, his face next to her ear, speaking urgently.

Emerson stopped in mid-chant. "I *knew* you'd try to save her." He gestured, and a latticed spirit cage formed around Black Fox. "Who's stupid now?"

Emerson grinned widely and turned to wade into the crowd of at least a hundred round demons on the warehouse floor. "Anyone hungry? I'm having a two-for-one special!" He pointed theatrically to Black Fox and Riya. The whimpering demon sounds turned to yowling as they struggled to get to their feet. "Stupid now!" chanted the demons. "Hungry!" "Special!"

Emerson seemed convinced the demons could make a meal of Black Fox. It was Idrián's fault that his grandfather was stuck again.

Surprisingly, Riya manifested an erasable marker and began rapidly writing something on the warehouse floor. She dropped the marker and began a complicated series of finger, wrist, and arm gestures that looked straight out of the pirated Indian Bollywood music videos his buddies used to watch in Iraq.

The floor under Black Fox's trapped figure turned transparent, then vanished altogether. Black Fox dropped like a rock. The empty spirit cage collapsed in on itself and vanished in a flash of ethereal light.

Riya hastily smeared what she'd written, and the hole disappeared.

Emerson was shaking with rage as he stalked toward Riya. "I'm going to rip—OW!" One of the round demons sank teeth into Emerson's left calf. Emerson kicked it off and threw it into several others. "Not me—the human!"

Yellow Snow, larger and faster, leapt over the front line of the round demons and into the clear circle where Riya kneeled, but its target was a disgustingly wet, congealed, brown mass on the floor that it ate while slashing and growling at a spiny, round demon that ventured too close.

A cluster of pale demons accidentally sent a work-light stand crashing to the ground, creating a hail of shattered glass. One demon tried eating the glass. Another chewed on the battery cable, shorting out the light and stunning the demon into insensibility.

Idrián pulled hard for more earth magic from beneath him, hoping the flow would be masked by the pandemonium caused by the awakened demons.

The first of the round demons got to Riya and tried to bite, but an arc of static electricity sent it flying into other demons, rolling them all backward like billiards. She got to her feet and backed up, putting her several steps closer to the west wall where he was concealed. Five or six more demons suffered the same fate before they learned to be more cautious. Each time they went flying, Riya moved westward, and their connection got stronger. She hesitated before stepping on the first ring of symbols, but luckily, the gate spell had exhausted their power.

Emerson viciously kicked the demons near him, then

spoke a word of power that pushed all eight of those around him backward into their brethren.

The demons closer to Idrián had no chance of getting to Riya or Emerson, and thankfully couldn't see him. They were more interested in fighting with one another, except he realized it wasn't violent, bloody, stabbing combat; it was sexual congress.

Some things were impossible to un-see, but Idrián planned to give it his best shot if they got out of this alive.

Emerson, toweringly angry, only got two more steps before nearly being knocked off his feet by Yellow Snow, who had made a grab for Riya and had been repelled by her spell.

Riya made it past the outer ring of the symbols. Another fifteen feet would put her into the shadows, beyond the pools of light.

Idrián needed to get the demons away from her. With an apology to the Spirit of Goats, he created a detailed illusion of an injured brown goat, complete with piteous calls and distinctive scent, and sent it to the southeast corner of the warehouse, as if it had wandered in by accident. His gamble that it would fool the new demons paid off, and they got in each other's way in their zeal to go after the new prey. Not enough of them, though. He added six more smelly, bleating goats and sent them to the southwest corner.

Emerson turned in response to the commotion. Idrián took the opportunity to extend his concealment spell over Riya. He moved closer to her, as much to use his stiffening right leg as to protect her. He'd need to be mobile once he got to her. A train rumbled in the distance to the north.

It was too much to hope that the demon inside Emerson hadn't noticed that much earth magic in its territory.

"Mage!" he howled. "Oath breaker!" He kicked at two more demons, but they were learning to avoid his feet. He spoke another word of power and cleared a space around him. Emerson started to run toward where Riya had been last, but her magic flared, and the floor under his feet was suddenly slick with black oil. He lost his footing and landed hard on his hands and knees.

Idrián half ran toward Riya as he sent the all the goat illusions running straight for Emerson. The round demons began converging on Emerson's location. "Mage!" "Special!" "Hungry!" They slipped and slid on the oily floor.

Riya made a beeline for Idrián. "West freight door!" He could barely hear her over the demon screams.

He turned and went into his top, half-run speed, using the spell he'd stored in his braid to light their way. Riya easily caught up with him and grabbed his free hand briefly. Their connection flared, and he felt her portal magic wrench open the west freight door, sending nails and boards flying. The screech from rusty metal even drowned out the demons. The building shuddered, and the noise in the room increased tenfold as a southbound train sped by.

She let go of his hand and sprinted forward, using her demon-repelling spell to clear the way for them both. Idrián risked a glance back and saw Emerson besieged by a mound of demons.

Idrián focused forward and blocked out everything but Riya and the west door.

A snarled word of power from Emerson rattled the walls and sent demons rolling past him like tumbleweeds. "Stop the portal mage!"

Idrián ignored it and ran. Up ahead, Riya stood at the entrance, holding out her hand for him. The wind from the train buffeted her, but she didn't budge.

He grabbed her hand and they leapt out the door together.

14

Rıya had never jumped next to a speeding train. It was a lot less scary in the movies.

They landed hard and fast, stumbling forward a few steps before getting control of their momentum. She was sure the only thing that saved them from a nose-first dive into the gravel was Idrián's earth magic, which she felt through their joined hands. How he managed to stay upright with a bad leg and a prosthetic foot was beyond her. Tiny rocks and debris stung her bare arms and face.

They rounded the end of the warehouse and staggered up the incline to the cracked asphalt parking lot. Idrián seemed to know where he was going, and she was happy to hang on. Only stars and Idrián's magic lit their way.

As they ran past a rusted hulk of a van, Riya magically sealed all the doors of the warehouse. It was too much to hope that the round demons would eat Emerson, but maybe the closed doors would slow them all down.

She and Idrián scrambled into his pickup truck. For all its battered exterior and aging upholstery, it started right away. He burned rubber out onto the deserted street, ignoring stop signs and potholes. She stomped on her bag to keep it from sliding and fumbled for the seat-belt. He turned onto a darker street and bore down on the accelerator. Somehow, he'd already strapped his seatbelt on. Maybe he had a spell for it.

His expression was grim. "I'm using the emergency translocation spell, but neither of us is going to like it."

She tried to kick her bag under her seat. "Better than being demon appetizers."

He gave her a fleeting smile as he gripped the wheel with one hand and leaned forward to pull a small knob hidden under the dash.

Burning bright lights and earsplitting thunder assaulted her as the truck went airborne and became a living ball of energy that hurled itself through space and time. Gravity failed, the temperature dropped, and she couldn't catch enough air to breathe. Her bag and every-thing in the cab began floating.

She caught glimpses of snowflakes, except they were stars marking clockwise paths, like a long-exposure photograph of the night sky. The contents of her stomach desperately wanted out, but she clamped her mouth shut and swallowed hard. She flailed her left arm, groping for Idrián's hand, but he was at the edge of the horizon, both hands on the steering wheel, shoulders hunched.

She hadn't even had a chance to say goodbye, or thank him for saving her. She moaned wordlessly, not daring to open her mouth to wail her regret at not telling him what was in her loudly beating heart.

Just when she thought they would die alone in the cold, airless space, a new bright light bathed the truck in fire and red dust and howling winds. Gravity returned, dropping the floating objects all around them. Thunder rolled, and they landed on a dusty dark road in the middle of a dark desert like they'd been shot out of a cannon.

The back end of the truck fishtailed wildly on the washboard ruts of the road. Idrián swore as he stomped on the brake. Once he got control of the vehicle, he slowed to a stop.

Riya's stomach rebelled, and she barely made it out of the truck in time to throw up on the side of the road. She heard similar retching from Idrián's side of the truck.

She staggered back to the open truck door and dug into her bag for a tissue to wipe her mouth. She pulled out two more, then dizzily staggered around the front of the frost-covered truck to where Idrián was still kneeling and wordlessly handed him the tissues.

"Passenger seat. Cooler. Water." He coughed as though he'd inhaled half the desert.

By the time she got back around to her side of the truck, she was feeling better— enough to give her hope that she wouldn't be nauseated and disoriented for the rest of her life. She shivered. Her filthy T-shirt and yoga pants weren't much protection against the cold night air.

After they'd each rinsed out their mouths and downed the rest of their bottles of water, he pulled her into his arms. She clung to him, letting the warmth of his body and their connection soothe her. She'd been terrified for hours, and never wanted to let him go again. In the distance, she thought she heard the hoot of an owl.

"Where are we, anyway?" She felt a lump pushing into

her stomach and looked down. "And why are you wearing my sweater around your waist?"

He released her with a chuckle "I thought you might be cold." He untied the arms of her sweater and handed it to her. She gratefully put it on.

"We're in southern New Mexico, a few miles from my family's ranch. This must have been the only road the translocation spell thought was safe." He looked to the east at the black, star-filled sky. "The spell bought us some time, but demons can translocate, too, and they can track anything. Now that we're back on Earth, they'll smell us, and the demon knows you're a portal mage. It'll want you back." He gripped her shoulders firmly, his expression determined. "It can't have you."

She wanted to kiss him for the fierce promise in his words, but there was no time. "Thank you."

She climbed into the driver's side of the truck and slid over to the passenger side. He clambered in after her, started the truck, and turned on the heater.

Once they were at speed on the bumpy road, she brought up a subject that had been worrying her. "You know that spell I did to free your grandfather? I, well, uhm... I don't know where I sent him. I was desperate, because Derorril was so confident the rolling demons could eat Black Fox, so I improvised. I didn't know what else to do." Anyone trained in magic knew that improvising was a good way to end up with very bad results, from sentient dust bunnies, to a Category Five hurricane.

He glanced at her. "It's okay, Riya." He reached out and grabbed her hand. "He wanted to go home, but I asked him to tell you about the dreamwalk powers first, which got him trapped again. You saved him." He stroked her thumb with his. "He's probably having an adventure."

She stole a glance at his profile, memorizing it for this moment in time. They weren't shifters, with the certainty of mate biology to move things along. They were just two humans with a talent for dreamwalk and a magical connection that warmed her from the inside out. She wanted to tell him…

The moment was lost when the "Infernal Dance" from Stravinsky's *The Firebird* began playing. She dug through the bag at her feet and found her phone.

"Hi, Mum."

Between dancing for demons, bending a demonic gateway spell, and taking a whirlwind tour of the universe via a kick-ass translocation spell, it seemed like a lot longer than thirty-six hours since she'd emailed photos of the magical symbols to her family. She'd already figured out some of them herself, sensing their meaning as her dancing had activated them.

She gave her mother a sanitized version of what had happened since, skimming over the dangerous parts and distracting her by mentioning that she'd met a very brave and handsome man, who she was with at that very moment. After providing his name, occupation, and assuring her mother he had no other girlfriends or wives, she steered the conversation to the magic symbols.

"Nasty," said her mother. *"A mix of necromancer, demon, and twisted dance magic. Your grandmother had a vision of the necromancer and looked him up. She's become quite the online research wizard. Spencer Emerson is the latest of a bunch of names over the decades. He makes a living on the stock exchange, but isn't above raising the dead to get juicy informa-*

tion for blackmailing the living. He used to have quite a fortune tucked away, but lately, he's been spending it like water."

"That's probably the demon that has him in thrall. It never met a resource it didn't want to waste. Idrián's people call them soul-eaters."

"Since you got away, maybe it'll try to find someone else to dance." Her mother sounded more hopeful than certain.

"If so, it'll kill them just like it did St. Peters. That gate spell won't work unless someone like me is powering it. The demon is greedy and arrogant, but it knows I'm its only hope for getting what it wants, which we think is to invite some of its family to town for dinner. Idrián is taking me to his ranch near Magic, New Mexico, which is more defensible than my place."

"Good. The folks in Magic will help you if they can. Necromancers know better than to go anywhere near that town, but the demon won't."

"Okay. Any ideas on how we get rid of the demons? I couldn't stop the gate spell altogether, but I misdirected it, so all that came through were little demons."

Idrián cleared his throat. "Tell her the little demons will eat any life force in their path, and that they're nearly indestructible." He shook his head and shuddered. "They also multiply like rabbits."

Riya relayed the information.

"All your grandmother and I can think of is sending them back through another portal. I've put in an emergency call to your father, and the minute he gets back to Earth, we're coming to see you." Her tone said there'd be no point in arguing.

"Looking forward to it, Mum." Riya loved her parents, but they still thought of her as their little fledgling, barely able to catch a field mouse without help. A short visit would probably be fine, as long as none of the rest of the family came along.

"Hold on a minute, dear...." Riya heard mumbled conversation in the background. *"Your grandmother says to tell you that the key to closing the gate is in the earth."*

Riya rolled her eyes at the prophecy that was no more helpful than the one Idrián's family oracle had provided. "Thank her for me, and I'll see you soon. Love you."

She told Idrián about the prophecy, what her mother said about Spencer Emerson, and what the necromancer said in the warehouse when the demon had temporarily left him.

Idrián's grim look returned. "Derorril's 'ride' is dying. All the more incentive for it to find you." He pressed down on the accelerator. "The wards on the ranch will slow him down, but they won't be enough."

She heard, or maybe felt, the despair in his voice, like he was blaming himself for something. She leaned toward him and put a hand on his blue-jean-covered thigh. Their ever-present connection amped up.

"We'll figure it out. I have faith in you. In us."

Riya didn't need a fence or a signpost to tell her when they crossed into the sacred lands of Idrián's people. One moment, she was alone in a dark truck with Idrián, and the next, she felt the watchful, wary eyes of dozens of spirits that powered the wards. Once past the perimeter, the land felt less forbidding and desolate than it had just half a mile back. It was impressively subtle protection magic to deter unwanted visitors.

The rutted dirt road took them along a fence, and finally to a crossroads, where he turned onto a smoother graded road that turned out to be the long driveway leading to the ranch's double front gate.

He used mundane remote controls to open and close the gates. Small solar-powered lights led toward darkened structures that she assumed were the ranch buildings. He drove slowly, then stopped. The headlights revealed a tan-colored mobile home with dark, curtainless windows, fronted by a small wooden porch.

An unexpected sense of comfort arose in her. She looked at Idrián and realized it was coming from him. He'd missed his home and his land.

He turned off the truck and switched off the headlights. "It's probably not what you're used to—"

"I camped in a tent and cooked over a butane stove in my warehouse for eight months while I was fixing it up." She unbuckled her seatbelt. "A mobile home looks pretty damn luxurious to me."

She started to open the door, but a flicker of movement stopped her. "Uhm, Idrián? There's a huge orange cat with flaming eyes and ears sitting on the fence post. Should I be worried?"

Idrián chuckled. "That's Necalli. She's just hoping you brought a few charcoal briquettes."

Riya grabbed her bag and got out of the truck. "Sorry, Necalli. I'll know better next time." She shut the truck door. The cat twitched her tail and yawned.

She walked to the front of the truck and waited while Idrián grabbed his bag and cane. In the stillness of the desert night, his brace creaked with every step he took toward the mobile home.

She waited for him to lead the way, then impulsively caught up with him and slipped her hand in his. Through their energized connection, she felt his deep, powerful connection to the land, like a network of underground power lines that radiated out to the wards. It was the feeling she'd been looking for her whole life, the one she'd started to build in her warehouse. "No wonder you love this place. You belong here."

He opened the door to the mobile home, switched on a light, and led her inside. A woven mat to the right of the door held a pair of dusty boots, one occupied by a prosthetic leg with a stars-and-stripes paint job.

She moved into the room a few steps. The décor was spare and eclectic. One corner of the living area had neatly arranged art supplies for the sand paintings he'd told her about. The furniture consisted of a mismatched but compatible work table, a small dining table and chairs, and a utilitarian kitchen, all in colors of sunrises and mountains. She liked the simplicity of it.

He shut the front door behind her, took her bag and set it on the floor with his, then wordlessly wrapped his arms around her in a long, tight hug. She relaxed into him and simply held onto his waist, feeling like time stopped for those few, precious moments.

"Welcome to my home," he said quietly. He kissed her so thoroughly that whatever she might have thought to reply dissolved in pure sensation.

Insistent waves of white noise arose from all around them. She broke the kiss to look for the source of the sounds. Idrián sighed.

He pulled back from her a little, looking at something behind her. "Yes, yes, all right." She looked around but didn't see anything but the door. She gave him a questioning look.

He slid his hands to her shoulders. "My ancestors want to meet you." His expression was apologetic, and his tone said he thought he was imposing on her.

"It's okay. I want to meet them, too." She smiled. "If it's any consolation, my family isn't any better at boundaries than yours seems to be."

The corner of his mouth twitched in amusement. He muttered a few words in a language she didn't recognize, then touched his index finger to her forehead above each eye. She felt the power of his earth magic through their connection with each touch.

Suddenly, the room she'd thought empty was filled with at least a dozen spirits, some overlapping, and more drifting in through the floor, ceiling, and walls.

Idrián touched her ears, and spirit voices began clamoring for her attention. She couldn't make out individual words or even languages. An overwhelming sea of sound filled her ears and head. She closed her eyes and tried to make sense of it.

"Enough!" bellowed Idrián. The clamoring stopped.

Riya opened her eyes and peeked up at him, then looked around the room. The spirit of an older woman in a brown skirt and pale blouse with a colorful sash around her thick waist drifted closer. She had the warmest smile Riya had ever seen. "I'm Juana Morales, Idrián's great-great aunt. I'll speak for us because I speak the best English. I hope you'll forgive us." She gestured at the other spirits that were all staring at her with frank curiosity or looking at their spectral feet. "Dreamwalk partners are uncommonly rare, and Idrián is our favorite living relative still here."

Idrián snorted in amusement. "I'm your *only* living relative still here." He gently urged Riya to turn so her back was leaning against him. "This is Riya Sanobal, my dreamwalk partner, and I am hers."

He patiently introduced her to all the spirits that approached. She gave up trying to remember any of the names, especially the complex ones in his ancestral language. She wanted to do better, but all she could think of was how he'd said he was hers.

Of all the moments to realize she was in love with the man, she couldn't think of a more awkward time than when meeting the ghosts of his powerful magical ancestors.

Idrián told the assembled spirits about the demons that were after Riya, and were very likely on her trail now.

"You must renew the wards," Juana said. "We can't hold the lands without them."

"I know, but how? They were keyed to Black Fox, and he isn't here to tell me how to change that."

"That man loves secrets too much, and now look where it's got us." Juana frowned in annoyance. "Usually, dreamwalk partners have weeks to work this out." She crossed her arms. "You and Riya need to bond and dance together at the nexus point for the wards."

Riya remembered the question she'd asked Idrián. "Does the dance have to be the exact movements, or is it finding his inner magic and peace through the movements?"

Juana beamed. "Oh, Idrián, bond with this woman

before she gets away. It's the magic. You have to dance both on Earth and in dreamwalk to unlock the wards, and you can only do that once you're properly bonded."

"What is 'properly' bonded?" asked Riya.

Juana's laugh sounded like a joyful, babbling brook. "You'll figure it out." She turned to face the rest of the spirits and made shooing motions. "We're all leaving now. Yes, elder, even you." She grabbed the ear of the spirit trying to hide under the table and hauled him out. The old man in the loincloth squirmed, then faded away. The other spirits left, leaving only Juana, who gave Idrián a meaningful look. "The new moon is a good time for planting seeds."

She melted like sleet into the floor and was gone.

Riya turned to face Idrián. "Did she just tell you we should be making babies?"

Idrián blushed, but stood his ground. "Yes, pretty much."

The idea didn't shock him as much as he once would have thought. It terrified him, but in a good way, because they'd be Riya's and his children, and he'd love them as much as he loved her. He wanted to tell her all that, tell her how he felt, and find out if she could love him, too, but the words bottled up in his throat when he remembered the wards and why they needed them.

She put her hands on his shoulders and looked up at him. She was heart-stoppingly beautiful. "I wish we had time to do this right, but those demons have to be stopped. If they don't come here, we'll have to go to them. We can't let them eat Denver. How do we bond?"

He tightened his grip on her. "It doesn't have to be us stopping the demons." He didn't want her anywhere near the Emerson demon, who would carelessly destroy her.

She shook her head. "It *does* have to be us. That's what the prophecies are about. I'm the key, remember? You're the earth." She rose up on her toes and kissed him softly. "Shifters describe mate bonding as two puzzle pieces snapping into place. Maybe with you and me, it's the blending of our magic. Finding the joy in dancing together."

She tasted so good that he returned her kiss with interest, then pulled her flat up against him and nuzzled her ear. "Maybe it has to be done in dreamwalk."

She kissed his chin. "Could we talk about this after you show me where the bathroom is?"

"Oh, sorry." He was rock-headed for not thinking of it sooner. "I don't have many guests."

Not willing to lose contact yet, he led by the hand past the kitchen, down the hallway with its solar-powered safety running lights, to the only bathroom, between the two small bedrooms at the back. He went back to the kitchen and poured two glasses of water, then drank one. Now that they weren't running for their lives, his body lodged multiple complaints about the bruises, scrapes, and muscles he'd strained in their escape. He'd come so close to losing her.

He scooped up Riya's bag and took it to the hallway just in time to meet her coming out of the bathroom. "I want to make love with you tonight."

She blinked in surprise, then beamed. "I want that, too. The sooner the better."

He nodded and led her into his small bedroom in the

back and switched on the dim overhead light. His unmade queen-sized bed took up most of the space. He put her bag on the floor next to the closet, then turned and pulled her into his arms and kissed her for all he was worth.

She kissed him back as she started pulling his T-shirt out of his pants. Her hands branded him with warmth wherever she touched him.

"I want to unwrap you like a present." He found the bottom edge of her T-shirt and pulled up.

She grabbed the hem herself and pulled it off over her head, taking her sweater with it. "Next time." She urged him to pull off his own T-shirt, which he did. She started on his belt, then hesitated. "Does your brace come off first?"

He swore under his breath. "Yes." He sat on the edge of the bed and worked the straps. She deserved more than a damaged man. His fingers slowed. Sooner or later, she'd figure that out...

"Idrián, look at me." The command in her tone would make a drill sergeant listen. "I want you, scars and all. This"—she patted his brace—"is no more important than freckles."

"Freckles?"

"Yes," she said, kneeling on the floor next to him and unbuckling the straps on his brace. "Girls with freckles think that's all anyone sees. Everyone else just sees a girl."

She helped him slide the brace off and lean it against the wall, then moved in between his legs and attacked his belt. The vision of her there sent blood racing to his groin, and his erection grew with each touch of her fingers, each brush against his thighs. The smile on her face said she knew the effect she had on him.

He stood and pulled her to her feet for a hard kiss, then boldly slid a hand to her breast and drew his thumb against her pebbled nipple. She moaned and arched into him. "Yes, Idrián. More."

He trailed kisses down her neck and tugged at the edge of her sports bra. "How does this come off?"

She leaned back and pulled it off over head, leaving him momentarily transfixed at the sight of her beautiful, round breasts with large, plump, dark nipples.

She cupped his face with her hands. "Get naked."

She didn't have to tell him twice. He was spurred on by the sight of her wriggling her pants and underwear down and tossing them onto her bag, leaving her tantalizingly bare before him, except for a small delicate chain she wore around her waist, and a thin strip of dark pubic hair. He eased his jeans and underwear down, freeing his erection, then sat on the edge of the bed to push them off his legs, only to realize he had to remove his shoes first.

He untied the right one and kicked it off, then ignored the left one and went straight for pulling off the prosthesis, then the liner. She took the liner from him and placed it on the homemade rack by his bed, then dug in her bag. How had he gotten lucky enough to find someone who took the daily realities of being with an amputee in stride? Her hands on his thighs focused him on her like a laser, and coherent thought flew out the window when she kneeled between his legs.

Riya glanced up at her sexy man to make sure he was still with her, then slid her hand up his smooth thigh and wrapped her fingers around his shaft to pump slowly. His breath hitched, and she smiled. She liked that he wanted her as much as she wanted him. She gave the head of his shaft a tentative lick with her tongue.

"No teasing. I'll come right here, and I'd rather be inside you."

His words made her core clench. She gave him one last pump, then crawled onto the bed and showed him the condom package in her hand. "Now or—"

He practically launched himself at her, pushing her onto her back and licking her upturned nipple, then closing his lips over it and swirling it with his tongue. Electricity raced through her and arrowed straight for her core, making her moan.

He switched to the neglected nipple, covering the first with his hand and rolling it gently. "So beautiful."

He settled on top of her, resting on his elbows, then slowly kissed down her belly. "I've been dying to taste you."

She wantonly spread her knees wide, trusting him as she'd trusted no other lover. "Please."

He slid his tongue between her lips and lapped upward, sending her hips thrusting toward him as he found his target. His tongue worked mortal magic and drove her near the edge in moments. He thrust a finger inside her, then two. She ground herself against him and grabbed her aching nipples. "I'm close…" He added a third finger inside her and flicked her clit back and forth rapidly with his tongue.

She cried out as an intense orgasm swept through her,

making her see pinpoints of light like the stars of dreamwalk. She reached for him blindly, wanting to hang onto him if the dreamwalk overtook them.

"Shhhh." He slid his body up hers sensuously. "I've got you."

He took the condom package from her hand and ripped it open. "I need to be inside you." He rolled it onto his beautiful male shaft.

"Yes, hurry." She covered her shakiness, and the seriousness of what they were about to do, with humor. "Your family's spirits won't stay gone for long."

Love swelled in Idrián's heart as Riya smiled. He knew he should give her more time to recover, but he couldn't wait any longer. He lined himself up at her entrance and pushed in gently, knowing she'd still be sensitive, but needing her heat more than he needed air. She gasped and spread her legs wider, the way only a dancer could. He thrust deep into her tight channel, and he was home. He stayed still to give her time to get used to him.

"Move," she breathed. "I want to feel you."

He retreated, then thrust in again, and after that, he couldn't have stopped for anything. He pumped hard and fast, leaning down for a quick kiss or to latch onto her tempting nipples. A tingling at the base of his spine said he was done for, and he didn't fight it. The rush of orgasm rolled over him like a power wave, roaring in his ears like the winds of dreamwalk. He was dimly aware that he shouted as he thrust spasmodically into her.

He opened his eyes and looked down at her flushed

face. The words that had stuck in his throat before came tumbling out. "I love you."

Tears leaked from her eyes, but she smiled. "I love you, too." She pulled him down to rest more of his weight on her. "This is going to sound crazy, but I think we need to dreamwalk. It's calling me."

"Me, too." He kissed her forehead. "We'll be glad later if we make ourselves comfortable here first." He reluctantly rolled off her and took care of the condom by wrapping it in a tissue. He shoved his naked stump into the specially lined prosthesis he kept by the bed, which was better than hopping one-legged or crawling to the bathroom.

He took the opportunity to brush his teeth and rinse the worst of the dirt off his face. It was a wonder she hadn't refused to kiss him.

He wanted a shower. If he was honest, he wanted a shower with Riya, but she was right. He felt the pull of dreamwalk like a constant refrain.

In his bedroom, Riya, still gloriously naked, was pulling back the sheets. She turned to watch him enter with unabashed admiration, giving his dick ideas.

He wanted her to know how happy he was, how perfect she was. All his dimwit brain could come up with was, "Bathroom's all yours."

She grabbed a small pouch from her bag and passed by him, but not before she kissed him. "There's a present under your pillow."

He turned on the bedside light, turned off the overhead, then sat on the bed and pulled off the prosthesis. The bedside clock said it was one in the morning. He was exhausted and exhilarated at the same time, and dreamwalk was insistent.

He lifted his pillow to see she'd left him a half dozen condom packages, lined up in a row. He made a vow to use every one of them with her, even though it would probably kill him. At least he'd die a happy man.

15

RIYA ENTERED THROUGH her sliding-glass door into summer and directly into her beloved Idrián's embrace. "Hi there, handsome." She kissed him. "Still loving the loincloth and the eagle's feet." She slid her hand onto his bare ass under the loincloth and squeezed gently.

He laughed and shook his head. "They're just legs."

She'd thought entering dreamwalk would solve everything, but all it did was make the pull stronger. She pointed toward the distant red lump that seemed to be the source. "Do you feel the call?"

"Yes." He took her hand. "I'll teach you speed travel next time. For now, just hang on."

It was as dizzying as ever, but at least it was short. Their destination turned out to be the graves of his ancestors, the windows face down in the mounds of red dirt. She remembered that to him, they were rocks. The call was almost shouting now, and she pulled Idrián toward the one mound that didn't have a window. It hadn't been there the last time.

"What do you see?" she asked.

"A pile of dirt." He shook his head. "I feel it. Like a rhythm in my chest of a song I should know."

Inspiration struck. "Dance with me." She felt his objection rise and put her finger on his lips to forestall it. "This is dreamwalk, where your potential isn't limited by what you think you can't do in the real world." She put his hand on her waist and put her hand on his hip. "Start with the impulse to move."

She swung her hips left and right, and gently pushed on his hip. "I'll mirror you."

He shut his eyes and began swaying. It was subtle at first, then more pronounced. The connection between them flared, and she felt a beat through him. She could lead him, but it wouldn't help. He would learn best by doing. "Teach me."

He began shuffling his feet left and right, tentatively at first, then with purpose and meaning. She matched him, movement for movement, step for step. His shoulders and torso moved in counterpoint, and she matched those, too.

Electricity built between them, wanting somewhere to go. She used her gift for opening doors to shape a key just for him and sent it to him over their connection.

His eyes flew open as he opened his arms wide. His feet stilled. His chest thrust up and out, like a dancer at the top of an arc. The electricity became a yellow beam that shot from his chest to blast away the red dirt to reveal a dark hole in the ground, with the top of a ladder sticking out of it.

He took a step closer, then held out his hand to her. "It's a kiva. I should have known. Come on."

"What's a kiva?" She wasn't liking the idea of climbing a rickety ladder into the unknown.

"Subterranean sacred room. My people borrowed it from earlier tribes to hide our treasure and our magic from the Spaniards."

She took a step back. "You go on. I'll wait."

He crossed to her and wrapped her in a hug. "What's wrong?"

"I don't like black holes in the ground. There aren't any doors." She shivered. "When I was twelve, my uncle trapped me in a well. It took my mother a day to find me because he used magic to hide it."

She felt the tension rise in him. "Why did he do that?"

"He's an orphaned condor shifter, the last of his kind. He refused to look outside his species for a mate, and he hated humans for the poisons that killed his kind. I'm mostly human, so..." She caressed the side of his face where his jaw tightened. "He's no threat. He's doing hard time in the cloud realm."

He stroked her hair. "If he comes anywhere near you, I'll kill him."

"You'll have to get in line behind my parents." She shrugged a shoulder. "That's why they're so protective of me." She sighed. "I'm going to have go in the hole, aren't I?"

"Like I said before, prophecies are hard on the people in them." He gave her a quick kiss. "I'll go first and turn on the lights."

Just as he stepped away, something invisible wrapped around her chest and yanked her backward, hard. "Idrián!" Her sliding door appeared and she sailed through it, barely missing slamming into the glass...

...She awoke in darkness, coughing, her eyes stinging from smoke pouring into the room. She shook Idrián's sleeping form, but he didn't respond. She remembered reading somewhere to get down low, under the smoke, so she wrestled his nude body onto the floor, wincing with each bruise she was sure she gave him. She used her magic to feel for openings and discovered one she hadn't noticed before, in the floor of the hallway. The windows in Idrián's bedroom were too high and small to be of any use, even if she could have lifted Idrián's inert body.

She pulled the coverlet off the bed and rolled Idrián onto it, hoping she wasn't about to make a dragging tarp out of a priceless heirloom.

Juana Morales flashed into view. "We're under attack. We were holding them off at the wards until the firecat flamed one of the small demons, and the big demon got mad and launched its burning body into the other end of the trailer. You have to renew the wards, or we'll be overrun."

"How do I do that?" She hastily pulled on her shoes, trying to take shallow breaths.

"Use the kiva below and connect with Idrián in dreamwalk."

Riya remembered something Idrián had told her. "Juana, invoke the treaty with Magic. They'll help."

Juana flickered like an old-time filmstrip. "We can't. It has to be someone living."

"Great," Riya grumbled. "No pressure." She knocked into something, and Idrián's wire frame prosthesis toppled into her. She grabbed it, the silicone liner, and his shoes and put them on top of Idrián's chest, along with whatever clothes she could find.

She found her T-shirt and wet it with water from a glass on the bedside table. She started to tie it around her face, then called herself a cloudbrain and used her dreamwalk skill to morph it into a wet bandanna, which made it easier to handle. If they lived through this, she was going to memorize a whole catalog's worth of safety equipment, starting with a firefighter's breathing mask. She morphed heavy jeans, a long-sleeve shirt, and hiking boots onto herself.

Foot by foot, she backed down the hall, sliding her butt along the floor, pulling the coverlet with Idrián. Adrenaline gave her strength, but made her shaky and wanting to pee. The walls made it easier to brace her legs for leverage with each new pull, but she couldn't see where she was going. She sensed the door to the kiva and used portal magic to brute-force it open. The trap door missed her by inches and banged against the wall.

She wiped her heavily watering eyes and looked into the opening. Attic-type stairs led down into inky darkness. Her involuntary gasp got her a lungful of smoke, which set off a fit of coughing that felt like it could break her ribs. If she didn't get Idrián down there, they'd both suffocate in the hallway.

Gritting her teeth, she pivoted on her butt and put her legs on the first step, then yanked on the coverlet to pull Idrián's shoulders onto her lap. His head lolled sideways, exposing the burned side of his face. He didn't need any more scars. She moved her feet to the next step down, then slid her butt down a step, pulling Idrián along with her.

Another step. She heard something fall in the living room and saw a flare of flame.

She yanked Idrián farther down with her. Something tore in her shoulder, but she could deal with that later. Another step.

Idrián's prosthesis slid off his chest into the darkness and landed with a soft thud. As soon as Idrián's legs cleared, she wrenched him further, then used her magic to close the trap door behind her. She hoped to hell there was some other source of oxygen in the kiva besides what came from burning trailer above.

Idrián's body started to slide downward on its own. She hung on and tried to protect his head as they bumped hard down six more steps. The darkness ate at her soul and terror had her teeth chattering in reaction. Where was a damn fear-eater demon when she needed one?

Two more steps, and her feet hit soft dirt instead of wooden stair.

She was alone in the bottom of a black pit with no way out.

Except she wasn't alone, and she wasn't a helpless child who hadn't come into her portal magic.

Idrián knew how to create magical light from the earth, so maybe she could, too. She reached for their connection and poured her need into it. Slowly, as if on a dimmer, lights came up in the room, which turned out to be circular, with a chair-height ledge all the way around. The center of the twenty-foot-diameter space had a bed of soft-looking, rich brown soil, and the whole room had a clean-earth smell. How perfect for an earth mage.

Now that she wasn't in a near panic, the dreamwalk call started again. Every muscle she owned protested while she dragged Idrián to the center of the room. In the earth light, she could tell she'd have some explaining to do about the scrapes and bruises on his body. Acting on instinct, she arranged him on his back so his naked skin had full contact with the soil. Even in comatose sleep, he was wickedly handsome. She smoothed his hair away from his face and wiped a smudge of dust from his chin.

Not knowing what else to do, she sat next to him, one hand flat on his chest, feeling it expand and release with each slow breath he took. She tracked the edges of his scars with her eyes, remembering the dreamwalk version of them that told a story of fire and rebirth.

From far away, and yet right behind her, she heard a voice calling her name.

"Idrián?"

The dreamwalk call swelled in her and brought her to her feet. She heard the beat that Idrián had in dreamwalk. She kicked off her shoes and morphed away her clothes, then began the dance Idrián had taught her in dreamwalk. With each step, sparks of electricity joined a mass of energy centered in her chest. When she got to the last steps, the stars of the Milky Way galaxy on a moonless desert night overlaid on the cozy world of the kiva. She had a vision of eagle-footed Idrián cradling her sleeping body in his arms, speaking words she couldn't hear.

The energy burst from her chest and shot into Idrián's at her feet. He arched up at the connection. In her vision, she saw a plasma ball of energy surround the images of eagle-footed Idrián and feather-haired Riya. Idrián in real life howled, and dreamwalk Riya keened, and they were suddenly fully awake, together, and aware.

Riya dropped to her knees and put her hands on his chest. "The wards," she told him. "Demons are attacking."

Because they were joined, bonded, on Earth and in dreamwalk, she felt his magic connect with the power of the earth, the strength of his ancestors, the sacrifices of his warrior ancestors who gave up their spiritual existence to become the wards of the sacred lands. The wards were thin in spots, scorched in others, barely holding. The sieging demons felt like blotches of creeping rot on white sand.

Idrián sent his warrior ancestors respect and honor. Dreamwalk Riya poured her magic into eagle-footed Idrián. Real-life Riya helped Idrián to sit up, and poured her love for him into their bond.

Fusion from above and heat from the deepest core below collected in the kiva, then shot out like a starburst, powering the wards to an all-consuming fiery brilliance that disintegrated any demon unlucky enough to be within twenty feet of them. The wards solidified and became whole. Riya saw a blocked tunnel that had to be the connection to the wards of the town of Magic. She called up her own magic and willed it to open. In her mind, the fallen rocks exploded away from the entrance and interior lights blinked on.

And with that, she was out of energy. All she could do was watch Idrián create a permanent connection to the deep earth to provide continuous power to the wards. The stars began spinning in earnest, like they had in the translocation spell. With her last bit of will, she threw herself against Idrián, so they wouldn't be separated again. Even though the lights faded, she felt his abiding love, and was content to sink into the darkness.

Idrián came to in his family's kiva with a full-body shud-der, caused by the emergency exit from dreamwalk, and the power of his newly bonded status.

Riya's form sprawled across his legs. He lifted her to a more comfortable position and cradled her in his arms, like he'd held her in the dreamwalk kiva. Dreamwalk Riya had called his name after he'd kissed her and started into the dreamwalk kiva, then had collapsed into an uncon-scious heap. He'd carried her down into the dreamwalk kiva, which turned out to be much bigger than the real-life one under his mobile home. Polished rocks at inter-vals in the rounded walls represented the graves of his warrior ancestors who'd become the wards of the tribal lands. He'd been honored and humbled when interacting with them to create the permanent connection to earth magic that would power the wards for as long as the planet lived. He would have stayed longer, but dreamwalk Riya faded as real-life Riya passed out.

Now all he needed to do was wake Riya and figure out how to rid the New Mexico desert of hundreds of vora-cious demons and one soul-eater that wanted Riya's magic. The good news was that, as near as he could tell, the demon occupying Emerson had translocated every last one of the smaller demons with it for the assault. It would make killing them easier.

The room smelled of smoke, so he used a bit of magic to renew the air as he took stock. He knew from foggy memories that Riya had dragged him out of the bedroom and down the stairs to the dark kiva. She'd been terrified, and yet she'd even remembered to bring his prosthesis and some clothes for him. She was the bravest person he'd ever known.

Hoping she was just sleeping because she was exhausted, he left her to rest on the soft earth while he crawled to where his leg and liner had dropped, beneath the stairs.

He used magic to clean the liner before putting it on and seating his stump. He walked to where the rest of his clothes lay and put them on. His stiff right knee felt surprisingly good, but he knew it wouldn't last. He took the coverlet to Riya to wrap her in, since she was buck naked.

She awoke as he knelt on one knee to lift her. "Hey, there," she said, then sat up and coughed like a three-pack-a-day smoker. "We kicked dreamwalk ass." She rotated her left shoulder and winced.

"We did, but we still have to kick demon ass." He held out his hands to her.

She groaned as she used him as a support to struggle to her feet. "Call Magic and invoke the treaty."

He nodded. "As soon as I find a phone." He stood.

She held her hand out to him. His cellphone materialized in it. "Call now. We need help."

He smiled and took the phone to send a text message, glad for magical women and modern technology. Out of the corner of his eye, he saw her change the coverlet into boots, jeans, and a T-shirt that said "Easily Distracted by Shiny Things" over an illustration of a starship.

"Can we ask Juana what's going on upstairs?"

"No. I banned the spirits from here, or I'd never have a moment alone." He put his hand on her left shoulder and felt the pain radiating through their bond. "I think I can fix this for you." Ever since waking, he'd felt a deeper connection with the healing power of the earth.

She smiled and caressed the side of his face. "I heal fast. I'll be okay in a few hours."

He climbed to the top of the stairs and touched the wooden trap door, then sent his magic throughout the mobile home. The west end was charred, but the rest of the structure was sound, if permeated with smoke. He used magic to spin the two ventilator turbines on the roof, sucking out the smoke and replacing it with clean air from the mountains. He spoke the spell to open the door.

Riya was right behind him as he emerged into the hallway. Juana Morales was waiting for him.

"Did we lose any of the animals?" he asked. "Patli?"

"None," said Juana. "Moyolhuani and Citlali herded most of them into the fireproof barn."

"Idrián invoked the treaty," said Riya, slipping her hand into his. Their bond hummed in his heart.

Juana nodded, looking relieved. "I'll tell the others." She blinked out.

The ground shook beneath their feet, and something exploded in the yard. "Dammit," muttered Riya. "Now what?"

16

I DRIÁN WINCED AS another screaming demon fireball arced over their heads and smashed through the fence. At this rate, it would take months to repair all the damage to the property.

Thanks to the unlucky accident that had damaged the mobile home, the soul-eater demon had discovered that burning round demons could breach the ranch's protections. It conjured a catapult and launched any demon it could catch, then used magic to set them on fire. The small demons died true deaths, but the earth told Idrián that more demons were being born even as their brethren died.

Idrián couldn't stop the fireballs, but he could create illusions that caused the soul-eater demon to misjudge the locations of the buildings. The southwest field looked like a battleground.

The love of his life scrambled into the cab of the pickup truck and shut the door. "Everything's set." She leaned over and gave him a quick kiss, then fumbled for her seat belt. "I like your friends."

"You could have just texted me," he grumbled.

She sighed. "We've been over this. The prophecies say both of us, and I'm not going to lose you again."

He knew all that, but he didn't like her being in danger. He started the truck and drove through the ruined gates, then turned north.

Their plan hinged on Derorril's greed and arrogance, both of which it had in spades, and the cooperation of the good citizens of Magic.

Idrián's oldest and most fearsome ancestor, a dark-skinned Mexica demigod who wore nothing but patterns of ochre and red paint, materialized between him and Riya. Idrián didn't understand the language he spoke, but one warrior always recognized another. He pointed east, counted out seven with his fingers, made a fist, then pointed east again, then made fists that appeared to leak blood. He vanished.

"I'm guessing either seven demons are already dead, or soon will be," said Riya.

"Seventy. They eat anything—plants, animals, insects —and when they have enough, they reproduce. Thank the spirits this land isn't a crowded city, but it'll take years for it to recover from the damage they've already done." The earth was crying out in agony already, and it hurt down to the marrow in his bones.

He turned east. The road here was little more than a couple of ruts, so their ride became bumpier as he raced toward the raised outcropping of red rocks. The truck's headlights cast strobing shadows on the dusty green sage bushes and a few roasted demon bodies as the truck climbed the hillock.

He stopped at the base of the smallest rock, grabbed his bag, and got out of the truck. Once Riya was safely out, he breathed on the side mirror to conceal the truck. He didn't want demons trashing it.

"I know these rocks," said Riya, looking around. "They're in dreamwalk, where I first saw you fighting the fear-eater demon." She tugged at his sleeve. "Come on, I'll show you the way up."

As he followed, he had time to marvel that she simply assumed he was capable of free-climbing rocks in the middle of a moonless night. Not even his grandfather had been able to see past his disabilities, and had waited until it was too late to teach Idrián about the wards and finding dreamwalk partners.

The rocks originated deep in the earth—perfect for what they had in mind.

She got to the top of the highest rock before he did, since he'd insisted on staying below her so he could use earth magic to catch her if need be.

"Uh, Idrián? I think we're going to need a bigger gate."

He crawled on his belly to look out.

A chaotic sea of hundreds of small round demons pressed at the bright wards, and spread out far beyond them. The land he could see was chewed bare of grasses and shrubs, with visible holes where the deepest roots had been dug up.

"We'll make it work. Are you ready?"

She swallowed, then nodded. He whispered a spell, and a flare shot up into the air from the west that formed into a firework image of a detailed M1 Abrams tank in the night sky.

Riya laughed. "Show off." She squeezed his shoulder, then stood up straight and tall. She wore a long, blue-gray duster that flapped in the wind.

"Yoo hoo, Derorril! Over here!" She waved her arms. A spell she'd readied made her sing-song voice echo far and wide. "Hell-o-o-o! Stupid demon who can't hit the broadside of a barn!"

The sea of round demons parted as Emerson strode through it. The round demons had apparently learned not to get too close, for fear of becoming another fireball.

"Stupid humans," snarled the demon, his voice magically enhanced to be heard. "I, Derorril, demand justice of the realms for the breaking of blood oaths. I will take the human known as Riya Sanobal in payment."

Idrián keyed his cell phone. "Go one, go two, go three," he said quietly.

Riya's derisive laugh rolled out. "You and what army? No oaths were given on either side. Onatecs lie just to get themselves up in the morning."

Emerson stomped, and the earth vibrated like a drum. "I will *show* you what army, stupid human!" From behind his back, spectral demon wings emerged and lifted Emerson off the ground. Raising one fist upward, he called down lightning from the cloudless sky, then pointed his other arm and channeled the lightning onto the ward fence, resulting in a cascade of sparks. Demons surged away from the burning embers.

Idrián spoke quietly into his cell phone. "Go four, go five, go six."

Riya put her fists on her hips. "That's it? Lightning?"

She laughed mockingly. "What do you think powers the fence, stupid demon?"

Even from this distance, Idrián could hear the small demons repeating "stupid demon."

Emerson landed hard on the ground. Derorril emerged from Emerson's body and shook itself as it stood taller and spread its wings. "You will pay!" It gathered power by sucking the life forces of the nearest demons, then sent the power directly at the wards.

The fence flared brilliant blue, then began to go dark in spots. The whole section in front of Derorril failed. He pointed through the fence. "Soup's on!"

A few round demons crossed without dying and immediate set about eating the first plants they came to. The rest of the demons saw it and surged forward. Miraculously, the human body that was Emerson wasn't trampled as it crawled toward the fence. That's all Idrián had time to see, because Riya had already materialized blocks and tackles and was rappelling down hers toward the natural half-circle of dirt below. He followed on his own without taking stops, using earth magic to cushion the landing. He turned to catch Riya on her last descent and carried her to the small flat rock on the edge.

"The symbols I gave you," she said. "He's coming fast."

Idrián used earth magic to etch the symbols onto the standing red rocks around them. She morphed her duster into black leggings and a tight T-shirt that said "Just Visiting This Planet" and began dancing. The symbols barely glowed at first, then brightened as every part of her moved at astonishing speed. He was so taken with her performance that he almost forgot to do his part.

"Now, Idrián!"

He created the illusion of a vast herd of ripe-smelling sheep, bleating in fear, all penned in by the rocks with no place to escape. Through the earth, he felt the small demons abandon the tough shrubs and head straight for the illusory sheep.

Outside the wards, he felt the thunder of ghostly cavalry horse hooves hitting the turf, driving the demons before them into the gap in the fence. Wolves, coyotes, and other unnamable predators howled, causing more demons to run toward the fence with their brethren. From the southeast, a mighty vibration rumbled through the earth, tumbling the rest of the demons into the gap.

When the last demon rolled through, the warded fence miraculously repaired itself, but none of the demons noticed.

Idrián fought the trembling ground to move as close to Riya as he dared, standing on the edge of the rock, then sank his hands into the vertical wall of rock and drew deep from the center of the earth. It was more power than he'd ever handled, and it made his bones ache. He gritted his teeth and sent the power into the rocks, where Riya's symbols absorbed it. The red dirt in front of them sank and became red, silver-streaked walls. Winds rose, then reversed with a pressure change that popped his ears.

He sent more power to the symbols, and more power to the sheep illusion, offering the tantalizing smell of fresh, soft lambs to the ravening demon horde.

The first wave of small demons tumbled into the open gate. Riya danced, and he channeled more power to the symbols. The gateway widened to the edge of the rocks and outward, sucking in round demons like a vacuum cleaner. Idrián added a herd of fat cows to his illusion, and goats, too, pushing the illusory smell outward.

"Stop! Stop! Stop!"

Derorril had discovered the trap.

It flew at the small demons, using sharp claws and its stinger tail to drive them back. Wherever the soul-eater passed, the illusion broke, but Idrián sent more constructs in to cover the gaps. Inspired by how successful Rollie and Hanif had been in scaring the demons into the gap, Idrián created a pack of hyenas at the back of the demon horde and made them howl like they'd found a dying wildebeest.

The more Derorril shouted and hurt the demons, the more they tried to dodge by running into the gate. Enraged, Derorril flew straight at Idrián and Riya with bloody intent in its scream.

From under and behind the ring of red rocks rose the spirits of Idrián's warrior ancestors, led by the Mexica demigod in full shift, with serpentine wings and huge eagle claws. Derorril tried to evade, but the demigod sank his claws into Derorril's chest and flew him high into the night sky.

Idrián felt Riya faltering and spared some power to share with her over their connection, but he was running out of steam himself. The gate's opening began to shrink.

The other warrior ancestors harried the rest of the demons into the gate, hunting down every last one of them and sending them over the receding edge.

Idrián looked skyward, trying to see what became of Derorril. They couldn't leave a soul-eater demon in the real world to wreak more havoc. Riya's movements dragged. He pulled his hands from out of the rock just in time to catch her.

"Dance with me," she whispered. "We can't stop."

He didn't know any dances. The gate continued to close. Desperately, he dragged up a dim memory from his childhood.

He touched his right hand to his chest, then stuck it out to the side, then touched his chest again. She matched him, just as she'd done in dreamwalk. He made a jazz hand and waved it, then took hers in his and gently turned her around in a circle clockwise.

He did the same movements with his left arm and turned her gently counter-clockwise. It was surreal, dancing with her in the maelstrom, and magical.

Just as he touched his right foot next to his left, he heard a high-pitched whistling sound, the kind made by an incoming missile. It triggered the hypervigilance he knew all too well, and he fought to hang on to the here and now, to block out the sensations that swamped his rational thought. And just as quickly, his thoughts smoothed out, and he felt warm and safe. He looked down at the feather-haired woman in his arms. "How did you know to take me to dreamwalk?"

"It seemed the right…"

He slammed back into his body with a jolt. Riya shuddered in his arms. She winced as the whistling sound resolved into screaming coming from straight above them. "Dance with me, Riya!" He hugged her tighter with his right arm and took a step to the side with his right foot. She did the same. He put his left foot next to his right, then put his hand on her thigh to urge her to do the same.

The hole was small, maybe the size of a wishing well, when Derorril's bleeding, ectoplasmic body slammed through the gate and vanished.

Riya sagged, and Idrián dropped to his knees to keep her from falling. The gate closed with a ground-shaking shudder.

The Mexica warrior landed on the sand, looking extremely satisfied. He raised his fist in victory and nodded to Idrián, then flew east toward the ward fence, where the other ancestor warriors were already headed.

Dawn was breaking to the east, and the whole world was quiet and peaceful. He was filthy, and every muscle in his body ached, but he couldn't bring himself to care. He'd found his dreamwalk partner, and they'd survived two prophecies.

He gently settled Riya into his lap.

She started shaking, and it took him a moment to realize it was with laughter.

He smiled, not knowing why. "What?"

She looked up at him with tired but bright eyes. "Your dance. We got rid of a killer demon from hell with the Hokey Pokey?"

He shrugged. "It's the only dance I know."

"It's perfect." Her smile was a balm on his battered soul.

EPILOGUE

Riya sat at the tiny café table in her dining room and sipped her favorite morning drink, a concoction of coffee, espresso powder, dark chocolate, and cayenne pepper she called "Wake the Dead."

Sunlight from the warehouse skylight warmed her, but not as much as the handsome, half-naked, dark-haired man standing in her kitchen, talking to his cousin on the phone.

"…but once we got Spencer Emerson into the ambulance, people from Magic were offering to fix the mobile home and the fence, and I wasn't going to turn them down."

The day they'd routed the demons, she and Idrián had been on their feet for thirty-six hours by the time they stumbled into his bed. They hadn't awakened for another ten hours, and hadn't gotten farther than a sleepy kiss when the ghost of Juana Morales dragged a protesting elder ancestor spirit out of the bedroom.

Idrián announced then and there he was driving Riya back up to Denver, loaded her in the truck, and took off.

"I'm being selfish," he'd told her. "I want to spend time with you without company or an audience."

She'd put her cards on the table and told him straight up that she wanted to live with him on the land that he loved, if he'd have her. She loved his ranch, the desert, his friends, and most of all, him. He'd demonstrated his enthusiasm for the idea by pulling into a rest stop, using magic to conceal the truck, then showing her how creative he could be with his hands, mouth, and body in tight spaces. She, in turn, showed him how flexible a dancer could be.

When they got into Denver, Riya's first call was to Whitney to find out how much creative fibbing she'd have to do to explain why she hadn't been at the theater when the firefighters had responded to the alarm and discovered the rest of the dancers. She was delighted to learn that the necromancer sleep spell had caused all the "gas leak" victims to forget the preceding three hours. All Riya had to do was say she'd become violently ill before rehearsal started and had spent the next two days fighting whatever had attacked her.

Whitney's bigger news was that she, Mack, Kenji, and two others dancers were leaving to form their own new company. Denise's treatment of Riya had been the last straw.

In the kitchen, Idrián's voice rose. "He did? Did he say where he's been?" Astonishment was written on his face.

Her phone played *The Firebird* ringtone, and she answered. "Hi, Mum."

"Hello, dear. Your father wants to know what time lunch is. He wants to visit the Butterfly Pavilion."

"We'll meet you in the hotel lobby at eleven thirty. Tell him no going misty and throwing off their humidifiers."

"I already told him. We'll see you in a few hours."

Riya's parents had arrived in Denver several days ago and demanded the full story from both her and Idrián. She'd already advised him to skim over the dangerous parts, or be willing to fend off pressing offers of unwanted security systems, bespelled guardian stone lions, and castle walls with moats full of deadly undines.

Idrián ended his call and brought his cup of plain, boring coffee to the table and sat. "Román says Black Fox showed up this morning in the living room of his new condo. He said he searched the galaxy and found the perfect woman for him." He shook his head in consternation, but she knew he'd been worried about his beloved, if exasperating, grandfather. She had, too.

Riya laughed. "Well, you said he liked doing the unexpected."

He smiled ruefully. "Román says it's my fault for making Black Fox think that he's now a matchmaker. And he's still irritated because I didn't read his email with the translation and gate-reversal spell until after the excitement." He ate the last bite of his croissant, which she'd bought yesterday when picking up her final paycheck from the coffee house. She'd made up for leaving them on such short notice by recommending one of her dancer friends who needed the work.

"It's a good spell. Unless he's the type to hold grudges, he'll get over it." She slipped her hand into his on the table and sent a pulse of her happiness through their bond. He smiled and caressed her fingers with his.

She took a deep breath. "Speaking of Black Fox, I've been thinking about a way to find dreamwalk warriors like he wants you to. It involves your ranch, but I don't want you to think I'm anything like that scorpion of an ex-girlfriend of yours."

He smiled. "Impossible. Tell me."

"I love helping veterans figure out how to move again after they've been injured. Opening doors and teaching them how to dance again. The land and your animals needed you on the ranch, and that motivated you to get stronger and find ways around your limitations. What if we could offer a program to selected veterans to help them do those things? Maybe we could ask the witches in Magic who designed that invitation spell to craft a very focused one for us, calling to people with dreamwalk potential who need the help and healing we can offer."

"I'd have to talk it over with the ancestors, but I'm intrigued." A troubled look crossed his face. "What about your dance career? You're really good. You should have more than me and the jackalopes for an audience."

"Thank you. I'll always be a dancer. I don't need a stage to do it." She smiled and squeezed his fingers. "Besides, our kids will need a home base, and I love the desert." She'd assured him last night that she'd wanted kids long before his ancestors started dropping heavy hints about new moons, planting seeds, and springtime births. He'd make a wonderful father, and their children would never be lonely with his ancestors around. And if her idea about a rehab center panned out, they'd have dreamwalk warriors to look out for them, too.

He stood and pulled her up into his arms for an embrace. "How about we get married today?"

Riya's heart filled to overflowing as she laughed and kissed him. "Why not? My parents and your family just happen to be in town, and it'd be a shame to waste a perfectly good marriage license."

"Not to mention making your grandmother look bad for predicting the wrong date for our wedding." He tenderly brushed hair away from her face.

She caressed the scarred side of his face with the drooping eye and deformed ear, and saw the precious man she loved with all of her heart.

"And if we're very, very lucky, that's the last prophecy about either of us for a very long time."

Thank you for reading **In Graves Below**, one of the stories in S.E. Smith's Worlds of Magic, New Mexico. I hope you loved Riya and Idrián and cheered as they fought demons, both from their past and those that wanted to make an appetizer out of Denver. I am grateful to Susan Smith for inviting me to play in her worlds.

If you like paranormal romance, check out the smokin' hot Ice Age Shifters series. Start with SHIFTER MATE MAGIC, set in 1993 and featuring a big bear of a man and a woman who's had bad experiences with shifters, and SHIFT OF DESTINY, set in present day, and featuring a prehistoric lion shifter and a woman convinced there's no such thing as magic, or sexy shifters. They're both standalone stories.

If you like science fiction romance, check out the Central Galactic Concordance series. It starts with OVERLOAD FLUX, where two strangers discover they must find a missing vaccine to save many worlds. There's a big damn space opera story arc going on.

SIGN UP FOR MY NEWSLETTER so you don't miss out on future books: bit.ly/CVN-news

Join my Facebook group, Carol Van Natta Author, for exclusive insider news and sneak peeks of future books, both paranormal romance and space opera romance. And right now, you can read the first chapter of SHIFTER MATE MAGIC next...

FREE EXCERPT FROM SHIFTER MATE MAGIC (ICE AGE SHIFTERS BOOK 1)

SOUTHERN WYOMING, SUMMER 1993

J ackie Breton needed to pee in the worst way.

Being five months pregnant meant stopping at every back-road truck stop and gas station, and sometimes behind bushes because her bladder was now the size of a damn walnut. Constant vibration from the motorcycle didn't help.

The faded billboard for Otto's Truck Stop, Take Next Right, enticed her, even though she really wanted to get through Cheyenne before it got too dark to find the highway that would take her east. Rural roads didn't have streetlights. She'd had her fill of dusty back roads and oblivious drivers in smelly diesel pickup trucks. A sharp kick from the baby inside her belly confirmed her decision. She slowed the bike and turned and was gratified to see her destination right away.

Otto's was bigger than she'd imagined, with dozens of long-haul semis, recreational vehicles, and pickup trucks in the sprawling parking lot. The crowd gave her pause, but not enough to turn away. She found a place to park near the front of the main building. The window decorations carried the western wildlife theme into the realm of kitschy, but she liked it.

As she deployed the kickstand and turned off the engine, her bladder spasmed, meaning she had to wait agonizing seconds for the urge to subside, or she'd leak, which would be too utterly embarrassing. She tightened her gloved fists on her thighs and willed the spasm to go away.

When she was sure she had control again, she took off her gloves and shoved them into her jacket pocket, then pulled the key and pocketed it, too. She stomped to get the circulation going in her unexpectedly rubbery legs as she took her backpack off the rail and shouldered it.

After a moment's hesitation, she slid her homemade weapon from the closest saddlebag into the pocket of her loose cargo jeans. Just because the brightly lit convenience store section seemed inviting and friendly didn't make it safe. She'd learned that lesson and so many others the hard way.

She pulled off the helmet, then slipped the re-snapped strap over her arm like a purse, albeit one with a hand-painted flaming skull. She'd been lucky to find a helmet close to her size in the thrift store. Its dusty face shield sported tiny scars from pebbles and splats from insects that would have been in her face if she hadn't been wearing it. The motorcycle's front fairing and windshield didn't block everything.

The ill-fitting leather jacket and heavy denim felt like a furnace now that she was standing in the dry summer heat of twilight, but she wouldn't be there long enough to make it worth her time to do more than unzip the jacket. She guessed she had forty-five minutes until sunset.

Outdoor speakers blared the upbeat country song about an achy-breaky heart. An errant breeze felt good on her sweat-plastered short hair, but the mixed smells of oil and gas threatened a return of the awful morning sickness she'd endured for the first sixteen weeks of her pregnancy. She hurried inside.

At the counter, she caught the attention of the clerk. "Restrooms?"

The bony blonde woman with too much makeup over her acne pointed toward the back. "Look for the orange signs. You gotta buy something if you use 'em."

Jackie nodded and walked quickly, following the arrows. Luckily, she didn't have to wait in line or share the facilities. After the blessed relief of peeing, she used soap and water from the sink to make herself look as presentable as possible under the circumstances. Her light brown skin already made her stand out, because the farther north she'd traveled, the fewer people she'd seen who looked like her. She threw the soiled paper towels in the trash and eyed herself critically in the mirror. At least now she didn't look like a dangerous fugitive who'd escaped a violent pack of leopard shifters who wanted her back alive or dead. Despite the warmth of the restroom, she shivered.

"Get back to the plan, Jackie," she told her mirrored self. She couldn't afford to fall apart, or everything she was afraid of would come to pass. She bent over to drink straight from the sink's faucet, then wiped the water off her face. She re-centered her her backpack and went out into the convenience store.

The smells of warm bread and sizzling hamburgers drew her like a lodestone toward the restaurant section, but she couldn't afford to waste the time or the money. She sternly made herself march into the back aisle and open the refrigerator door for the lunch meats and cheeses.

She got a whiff of a tantalizing scent as she pulled her selections off the hooks. Not food, but something intensely interesting. Her sense of hearing and smell had magnified with each passing week of her pregnancy. She wished she knew if that was typical for a human woman carrying a shifter's child but she had no one to ask. Certainly not the lying son-of-a-bitch leopard who'd gotten her pregnant, despite her precautions. She hoped he was roasting in hell, but he probably wasn't. Justice for the privileged rich, regardless of skin color or species, had a whole different set of rules.

She let go of the refrigerator door and turned toward the scent, only to run headlong into a man who'd just turned down the aisle.

"Sorry," she said, even as he said the same word. She regained control of her suddenly clumsy feet. She got the impression of chiseled cheekbones and a square jaw before she dropped her gaze out of habit, one learned from living with volatile shifters. His scent hit her like a freight train a moment later, all woodsy and leathery and mouth-wateringly male.

No one, not even the father of her baby, back when she'd thought she was in love with him and he with her, had ever smelled that good. She took a step back, because if she hadn't, she'd have been tempted to stick her face in the vee of his short-sleeved T-shirt and lick.

"My fault," he said. "Are you..." He trailed off and audibly swallowed.

She made the mistake of looking up at him and confirmed that he was the sexiest man she'd ever seen, even counting the handsome actors she'd thrilled over as a teenager. His brown skin and features spoke of an ethnic heritage something like hers, and his warm, coppery-brown eyes threatened to drown her on the spot. His wide shoulders and arms looked strong enough to protect her from anything. The few tight coils of hair on his muscled chest mirrored the close-cropped hair on his head. His low-slung jeans and boots completed the mesmerizing package.

She swallowed and took another step back, away from temptation. "I'm fine."

Except she wasn't. She wanted to set fire to all her plans in favor of getting to know the man standing in front of her. For his part, he looked stunned.

She shook herself. Not, not, not happening. She was a pregnant fugitive with enough secrets to write her own soap opera, and an implacable enemy on her tail. A human, no matter how tall, broad-shouldered, and sexy, was no match for a criminal cat-shifter pride with claws and teeth, and vengeance on their minds.

She clutched her meat and cheese packages to her chest and turned away, even though her now throbbing body and aching breasts begged her to get closer. She'd learned to ride out the hormonal roller coaster of being pregnant, so she could damn well ride this out, too.

She made her way to the register, then realized she'd forgotten milk. Before she'd gotten pregnant, she'd been allergic to the stuff, and she still disliked it, but carrying a leopard-shifter's child made her crave it, so she compromised by drinking chocolate milk whenever she could.

She left her purchases on the counter, ignoring the blonde clerk's irritated look. Better that than having the woman accuse Jackie of shoplifting. Been there, done that, had the long wait for the cops.

She ignored her impulse to find Mr. Broad Shoulders again and walked to the other side of the store where the drink coolers took up a whole wall.

Two men who looked enough alike to be brothers were arguing in front of the beer case. They wore loose, motorcycle-club leather vests over their dusty jeans and T-shirts and stank of stale sweat and belched beer.

The taller man pulled the six-pack of yellow cans out of the shorter man's arms and shoved it back in the case. "No way am I drinking that swill." He grabbed a carton of brown bottles and shoved it into the other man's arms.

The shorter man shoved the carton back into the other's hands and grabbed the cans again. "I'm not pissing Dad off. You can fucking buy your own."

Jackie hesitated, then told herself just to get her milk and get out. She marched to the door, opened it, and grabbed the first chocolate milk carton she saw. Her baby picked that moment to kick hard and sharp. "Shouldn't have watched that kung fu movie last week," she muttered toward her belly.

"Hi, there, foxy lady. I'm Wiley."

She flinched in surprise. Somehow, the shorter man with the dark eyes and thin mouth had snuck up on her and was standing close enough to grab her.

"Your face'd be prettier if you'd smile." He was only a couple of inches taller than her five-foot-eight height. He scented the air like a dog. "Damn, woman. You smell fucking great." His eyes narrowed, and his focus intensified.

She backed away, fear rising. Only shifters noticed her scent like that. She couldn't help it that she smelled like a sexy baby factory to shifter males, even when she was pregnant. It was just her luck to run into shifters in an all-night truck stop. She'd had enough of the lazy, greedy breed to last a lifetime.

"Back off," she said firmly, dropping her arm so her helmet's strap slid down her forearm into her waiting hand.

The taller man came up behind Wiley. "How much for a BJ?"

It took her a moment to realize he thought she was a truck-stop prostitute. "Not for sale," she snapped. She'd take time to be outraged later.

She backed up another step, but Wiley grabbed her arm. The movement knocked the milk carton out of her hand. The carton bounced once and began leaking.

The taller man eyed her stomach and sneered. "Every-thing's for sale if the price is right. Fat girls like you oughta be grateful for what you can get."

Her jaw dropped. *Fat girl?*

The taller man weaved a little and reeked of alcohol. It took pounding down a lot of hard liquor for a shifter to get drunk. He scented the air, and his smile turned feral. "We'll show you a real good time."

Her fear and anger spiked. "I said no!" She stomped hard on Wiley's instep, then kneed him.

He buckled in pain. Not even shifters were immune to nut shots.

She pivoted and ran toward the bathrooms where she'd noticed a back door. Adrenaline gave her feet wings.

She heard curses behind her as she rounded the corner into the hallway. She hit the door's exit bar at top speed and burst through it into the wide alley. The buildings cast darker shadows at dusk. She stumbled as she lost traction on the dirt and gravel, but recovered and took off to the left, away from the multiple trash bins and toward the well-lit asphalt parking lot. Maybe she could get help from some of the truckers.

She'd almost made it to the pavement when she heard pounding footsteps and growling behind her. Acting on instinct, she veered right, then used her momentum to spin around. She bashed the tall, drunk man on the head with her helmet.

He staggered and fell to one knee. "Fuck!"

She launched into a run, only to get jerked back when he grabbed the back hem of her jacket. She spun sideways, out of his grasp, and swung at him again with the helmet.

He blocked it with his forearm, then ripped the helmet from her grasp and threw it away.

She backed up.

He clambered to his feet and smiled. "Feisty! I like that." He reached out long arms to corral her, but she dodged away.

She fumbled in the pocket of her cargo jeans and pulled out the slender, rusty pipe, then powered it.

From the back doorway, a big dog—no, a coyote burst out and landed. It trotted straight for her. The coyote was larger than its animal-world counterpart, as some shifters were.

The tall man grabbed for her again.

"No!" She thwacked his exposed wrist with her pipe. A blue spark flashed. He jerked back and howled in pain. She jabbed the pipe into his stomach.

He fell sideways and spasmed like he'd been hit with a cattle prod. Which he had, after a fashion, because that's what the magic she'd stored in the tube did.

The coyote slowed and stalked toward her, growling with yellow-eyed menace.

She took a swipe at his muzzle with her tube. "Back off, fur butt!"

She felt something on her leg and looked down just as the tall man's hand clamped around her ankle. He growled through temporarily distorted teeth. Shit, he was changing right there, in almost-public, without bothering to take off his clothes. The first coyote lunged forward to grab her forearm. She shrieked, but her husky voice had never been very loud. She pushed her forearm into his mouth to make him gag and back off, grimly hanging onto her pipe.

A huge, rounded shadow emerged from the other end of the alley, near the trash bins. It barreled toward them with a roar loud enough to reverberate off the brick walls.

The coyote spun to face the new menace with a snarl.

The taller man finished shifting and shook off the shreds of his pants and ripped vest. The remnants of his T-shirt looked like a cheap collar.

She backed away, intending to run, but found herself unable to take her eyes off the largest, shaggiest bear she'd ever seen. Not that she'd seen one up close before. It was as big as a diesel pickup truck and had distinctive pale markings across its furry nose and chest.

The first coyote darted sideways to slash sharp teeth at the bear's throat. The bear ignored him as it swung a mighty paw at the T-shirt coyote, knocking him back a good ten feet. T-shirt coyote slowly scrabbled to his feet, shaking his head as if dazed.

The other coyote danced back, and then in again, biting the bear's shoulder. The bear turned and snapped wickedly long teeth at the coyote. He nimbly dodged away.

The T-shirt coyote lunged forward and bit at the bear's other shoulder, but only came away with a mouthful of shaggy fur. The bear growled and swatted the T-shirt coyote again. This time, he flew through the air and hit the brick wall of the store hard with a pained yip, then fell to the ground.

The bear turned to snap at the other coyote again. The coyote scrambled backward, then lunged in and bit the bear's flank.

The bear sat on him.

The squashed coyote whined, then was silent.

She glanced at the T-shirt coyote, but he lay unmoving in the dirt.

A powerful wave of something indescribable buffeted her senses, sort of like magic, but not. It seemed to come from the bear, and felt like an imperative to do something, but she didn't know what.

Her brain managed to get a coherent thought past her shock. If the huge bear shifter with equally huge claws thought she smelled really good, she'd have no chance at all of getting away. Fear galvanized her into backing up with tiny, shuffling steps. Maybe he wouldn't notice...

The bear whined, and she froze.

The massive animal heaved itself up and forward. Even as she watched, the flattened coyote was shifting back into a naked man. He was out cold. A quick glance toward the wall told her the other shifter was now human, too, wearing nothing but the ragged T-shirt collar.

The bear took a step toward her.

She trembled with the need to run but running prey excited predator shifters. She couldn't help the whimper of fear that escaped her.

More not-magic brushed her senses, this time like a velvety soft blanket against her skin.

In an instant, the bear became a fully clothed man wearing jeans and a V-necked T-shirt over a hundred yards of muscles. Mr. Broad Shoulders himself.

Of course, the hottest man on Earth would turn out to be a shifter.

"Are you hurt?" His tone matched his worried expression. Even his voice made her want to step closer so he could whisper in her ear.

"No, I'm fine." Her baby took that moment to kick, and she winced.

He took one small step forward. "You're in pain."

"It'll go away." She darted her gaze away for a moment to look for her helmet. "Thank you for helping me." She kept her eyes on him as she took a trial step away, to see how he reacted. When he did nothing but stand there, with worry tightening his wide, kissable mouth, she moved slowly toward her helmet, watching him the whole time. Her makeshift magic-powered pipe needed recharging, so she slid it into the pocket of her cargo pants before bending over to pick up the helmet.

He cleared his throat. "Could I, er, buy you a cup of coffee?" His tone almost sounded shy.

Yes, yes, yes, sang her body, suddenly flush with raging hormones. She almost swayed toward him.

No, no, no, shouted her rational brain, the one that had plans. The first and only time she'd listened to her body, she'd ended up pregnant and an unwilling captive of a feline-shifter pride.

"Thanks, but I'm already running late." She sidled toward the asphalt edge of the parking lot. It felt wrong to move away from him, but her situation made anything between them impossible. "I'm truly grateful for what you did." She tilted her head toward the men lying in the alley. "Shifting in public like that means they're fur-brained fatheads. Neither of us should be here when they wake up."

"Let me at least walk you to wherever your bike is parked." He pointed a thumb toward the convenience store's back door. "They may have buddies."

She hesitated, then sighed. "Okay. Thanks." She should have thought of that. Asshole shifters always had buddies.

She stepped up onto the asphalt. He put his hands in his pockets and rounded his shoulders, as if trying to make himself look harmless. He failed miserably, because it drew attention to his low-slung jeans and made her wonder what he'd look like without them. She'd bet her motorcycle he'd look a damn sight better than two scrawny coyotes.

They walked quietly together as the parking lot's

lights blinked on. His mother must have brought him up right, because he matched his stride to hers and kept a respectful distance. She allowed herself the secret, impossible fantasy that he was her man and she was his woman.

"Do you have someone you can call?" He glanced at her stomach, then away. "A mate, maybe?"

"No, thank God. I've had quite enough of shifters for a while." Realizing what she'd said, she added hastily, "Present company excepted."

He shrugged one shoulder, but his mouth twitched with humor. It gave her the wild impulse to do whatever it took to see him really smile, because she just knew he'd be stunning. And she shouldn't be having those thoughts. She was a total basket case.

The sun dipped to touch the highest mountains to the west just as they arrived at her motorcycle. It looked lonely, standing by itself.

She shook off the fantasy, then looked up into his beautiful coppery eyes. "Thank you again."

"I was thinking." He tightened his hands into fists in his pockets, making his arm muscles bulge. "My semi only has half a load in the trailer. I could put your bike in there and take you someplace safe for the night."

She shook her head. "That's a gracious offer, but I need to keep moving." She zipped up the jacket to prevent it from flapping in the wind and turned the kerchief at her neck around, so she could pull it up over her mouth to protect against road dust.

His eyes darkened. "If you're in trouble, maybe I can help."

He was making this so hard. "If I were in trouble, it would be horribly unfair of me to drag you into it, after you kicked coyote-shifter ass for me." She fished the key out of her pocket and put it in the ignition.

"I wouldn't mind." His resolute expression hinted at stubborn determination. He glanced to her stomach again. "You shouldn't be unprotected."

She appreciated his tact. He'd obviously figured out she was pregnant. Shifters could scent that kind of thing immediately. The coyotes should have noticed, but they'd been too drunk on high-test booze and shifter-mate lust.

"I shouldn't be a lot of things, but here I am." An absurd thought crossed her mind, and her eyes went wide. "Oh my God! The name of the shifter you sat on was Wiley. You sat on Wiley Coyote!" She almost doubled over with laughter. It felt like forever since she'd found anything to laugh about.

His wide grin was every bit as sexy as the rest of him. "He must hate those cartoons."

Still chuckling, she undid the helmet's strap. "I'll remember seeing that for the rest of my life." She hoped he'd think she meant his bear form sitting on the coyote, and not his amazing smile that would be etched in her memory forever.

She dusted off the faceplate on her pants, relieved to find it not even scratched. She pulled the helmet on and secured the strap under her chin.

He pulled his wallet out and handed her a card. "This is me. That number is for a cellular phone that's in my rig. If you ever need me to sit on someone, or you just want to talk, I hope you'll call me."

She took the card and read the top line out loud. "Trevor Hammond Independent Trucking." She put the card safely in the zippered pocket over her chest. "I'm

Jackie Breton, by the way. Well, Jacqueline, but only my mother and my former boss called me that." That was another life, one she could never go back to. She pulled out her gloves and put them on.

"Nice to meet you, Jackie." He stepped back. He looked as deeply unhappy as she felt, but that didn't make much sense. He was a big, strong, healthy bear shifter, with wicked-long claws and magic, not an almost powerless, pregnant, terrified human on the run.

She straddled her bike and rocked it forward, letting the motion close the kickstand. She started the engine, gunned the hand throttle enough to make a slow circle, then straightened out and headed for the parking lot's exit. She briefly lifted one hand and waved in case Trevor was still watching.

She liked the sound of his name. Hell, she liked the sound of everything about him, not to mention wanting to rub herself over every inch of him, even though she hadn't been force-changed into a feline. If her life ever got normal again, maybe she would call him.

She shook her head. Her life was not *Last of the Mohicans*, with her handsome savior telling her to stay alive and promising that no matter where she went, he would find her. It was more like *Marked for Death*, where she'd be lucky to survive the vindictive people after her.

She squared her shoulders and got back to her plan. It was her best shot at staying alive. Probably her only shot.

Read the rest in <u>Shifter Mate Magic</u>